The Cherry Trees of Rosings

A PRIDE & PREJUDICE VARIATION

MORGAN BLAKE

SIGN UP TO RECEIVE
AUTHOR MORGAN BLAKE'S NEWSLETTER
BE THE FIRST IN THE KNOW
ABOUT BOOK RELEASES,
GIVEAWAY BOXES & MORE.

ALSO AVAILABLE:
(SUBSCRIBER EXCLUSIVE DOWNLOAD)
LIZZY X DARCY
NOVELETTE

WWW.MORGANBLAKEAUTHOR.COM

Contents

Author's Note

D ear readers, I hope you enjoy reading this book as much as I loved writing it.

And don't worry about spooky stuff! The story may have a supernatural bend, but it is comical for the most part (and a tear-jerker in other parts). It is the mystery our dynamic duo shall try to figure out through the course of the book.

A small note on spellings: I have used British English spellings...outside of a few places. But I have retained the "Mr." and "Mrs." tags as that was the Regency Era style.

Finally, I would like to give a shoutout to my lovely alpha readers Lynne, Nicole, and Jessica. Your thoughtful comments and suggestions helped shape 'The Cherry Trees of Rosings' to what you have in your hands now. Three cheers!

MORGAN BLAKE

Book Playlist

- *A Flower amidst Thorns —Joshua Kyan Aalampour*

- *Prelude & Passacaglia —Karim Kamar*

- *Valse Sentimentale No. 2 in G Minor —Eric Christian*

- *Solas —Jamie Duffy*

- *Glimpse of the Past —James Quinn*

- *I Love You —RIOPY*

- *Starry Night —Jordan Critz*

- *Butterflies (Piano Sonata) —Tony Anderson*

- *rises the moon - liana flores —Birru*

- *Truth —Dylan John Sparkes*

- *Waterfall —James Quinn*

- *Vivaldi: Summer / The Four Seasons —Kassia*

- *Idea 20 —Gibran Alcocer*

- *Ethereal (slowed) —Txmy*

- *Time (original) —Tony Ann*

- *Idea 7 (Slowed + Reverb) —Gibran Alcocer*

- *Passion —Gabriel Albuqurqüe*

- *Novella —Jordan Critz*

The Cherry Trees of Rosings

A PRIDE & PREJUDICE VARIATION

Chapter 1:

An Eerie Encounter

E lizabeth Bennet had only been at the Hunsford parsonage for three days when she saw Mr. Darcy under the cherry trees.

Her heart raced—a quick *thump, thump, thump!*—as she sped off the walking path to hide behind an ash tree. *What was Mr. Darcy doing at Rosings?*

That was when she remembered: he was the esteemed nephew of Lady Catherine de Bourgh.

Elizabeth had yet to meet the benefactress of her cousin, Mr. Collins—though he spoke of her in practically every sentence, of every conversation, every day. She was certain one would not find a more devout champion of any patron anywhere in the lands if they tried. But she would not have to wait much longer to satisfy her curiosity about the lady. After all, they had received an invitation just that morning to present themselves at Rosings for tea.

Elizabeth glanced at Mr. Darcy from around the trunk of the ash tree. It appeared she had one less surprise waiting for her in those quarters.

She quickly turned around and started off on a different path for her morning walk.

The way she saw it, there was no need to inconvenience the gentleman with frivolous civilities and hellos. He would surely be the last person to welcome such overt social mores.

Later that evening...

Elizabeth finished arranging her hair in a simple fashion before stepping out of her room. The rest of the inhabitants of the parsonage were already at the foyer of the cottage.

"Hurry along! Hurry along! Charlotte, Sister Maria, Cousin Elizabeth!" Mr. Collins called. "We must not keep her ladyship waiting!"

He was sweating profusely. Perhaps at the thought of arriving a few minutes late and having to prostrate at his patroness' feet. Elizabeth coughed into her hand to cover her smirk as she joined them.

"Oh! What was that?" Mr. Collins asked, turning towards her. "Cousin Elizabeth, are you unwell?" He looked comically red in the face. "Perhaps you should stay behind. Her ladyship has strict rules about bringing disease into the great house!"

Elizabeth barely restrained herself from rolling her eyes. Though she did arch her eyebrows in amusement.

"I think I swallowed some dust. Nothing to worry about surely."

"Dust? Did you say dust?" Mr. Collins' eyes widened. He turned to his wife. "Charlotte! You must tell Mrs. Bishop to be more meticulous! I cannot have her humiliating me if her ladyship visits one day and sees such deplorable state of affairs. You know how..."

Elizabeth tuned out her hapless cousin's words. It was surely an irony that the man had a housekeeper named Bishop—one who had arrived at the recommendation of Lady Catherine herself—while he worshipped nobody higher than his patroness. She only hoped that Charlotte would not be too vexed at her for stirring up Mr. Collins' humors.

"Mr. Collins, I assure you," Charlotte said, with the patience of a saint once her husband stopped to catch his breath. "I have matters well in hand. Perhaps we should start for Rosings if we wish to arrive on time."

"Yes, yes, at once!"

The party soon left the cottage.

...and reached Rosings, right at the dot of four o'clock.

It never failed to amaze Elizabeth how Mr. Collins managed to arrive everywhere at just the precise hour. But she could not ponder on it too long as they found themselves following the butler (rather briskly), as he led them to the west parlour of the house, where her ladyship was to be found. Though, she did notice—along the way—how unerringly accurate Mr. Collins had been in his description of all the interiors. Right down to the number of stained glass arches above every window set!

"And there, you see, right beside the doors are the prized suits of armour that were gifted to Sir Lewis de Bourgh during his lifetime. By the Earl of Nottingham, no less!" Mr. Collins announced helpfully. "Her ladyship prefers the light in this particular parlour at this time of the day. But not when her gout is acting up."

A steady stream of commentary on such matters had accompanied them all the way from the gates of the parsonage. And it did not appear Mr. Collins would stop anytime soon.

Elizabeth eyed the armours. They were polished to a shine and clearly well-maintained. So much that she wondered if they might spring to life any moment. But her attention was soon drawn away.

Because, just then, the butler pushed open the grand doors of the parlour and held up a hand for them to wait.

He walked in. Nose in the air.

"Mr. Collins and Mrs. Collins are here, your ladyship," he announced. "As are Mr. Collins' two relatives."

Elizabeth felt her eyebrows arch at the excessive ceremony. Then she wondered if she would find Mr. Darcy inside, sitting beside his aunt, and possibly his cousin. All their noses high in the air. Collective disdain palpable at the substandard guests about to enter their inner sanctum.

Her lips twitched into a grin.

"Yes, send them in!" A loud—slightly shrill but decisive—voice boomed out from within the parlour.

It startled Maria Lucas. Enough that she clutched at Charlotte's arm. But there was no time to offer any reassurances.

They were now very much within the lioness' den.

Chapter 2:

No Green Beans

"**M**r. Collins, you know how I despise green beans!"

Lady Catherine's brows drew down with annoyance as she looked over the tiny list Charlotte had handed her a few moments ago. It was about the gift baskets the Collinses were tasked with distributing for Easter; one of the yearly tasks of the parsonage.

"You *shall not* present that vegetable to the congregation," she emphasized, mouth twisting into a moue of distaste.

Mr. Collins nodded his head vigorously. "Indeed, your ladyship."

"Potatoes will do very well. Very well, indeed..."

More head nodding from her cousin.

Elizabeth held back a chuckle as the spectacle unfolded before her.

She had been somewhat right in her estimation of Lady Catherine from Mr. Collins' extensive effusions. But once the introductions were made, she was pleasantly surprised to find that the great lady was even more ridiculous than she had imagined. Her father would be dearly entertained by such human folly once she wrote to him.

"Potatoes are vegetables for the hard-working," Lady Catherine continued sagely. Then she picked up a cream tart from the platter before her and bit into it.

"You are quite right, your ladyship, as always," Mr. Collins said. "I merely wished to place the beans in the baskets for the sick—"

"You should speak on the virtues of potatoes in your sermon, Mr. Collins," the lady said, dusting off the crumbs from her fingers before fixing a glare on her parson. "Remind them of their good fortune and the evils of laziness."

Elizabeth discreetly watched as a stray crumb held on to dear life against the whiskered mole to the side of Lady Catherine's mouth. The one to the left of her beaked nose.

"Mrs. Collins, you may ask Mrs. Stone to give you some of the dried orange peels she is making with Jenkinson. A little bit of colour will not be unpious in an Easter basket. Mr. Collins, you must remind the congregation to keep their homes clean and take baths regularly…"

Yes, Elizabeth would have to write to her father soon.

But there was one thing that surprised her greatly that evening.

Mr. Darcy never appeared.

Not once.

Nor did his aunt mention him outside of one lengthy diatribe on how he and Miss Anne de Bourgh, Lady Catherine's daughter, were made for each other. And that he needed to hurry up and do his duty by his family by marrying her.

It confused and perturbed Elizabeth.

Did the man consider himself so above them that he could not be bothered to join them for tea?

Or... was she mistaken about who she had seen earlier that day?

The next morning, when Elizabeth neared her favourite walking path, she was startled to see Mr. Darcy under the cherry trees once more.

The blossoms were gently floating around him, falling out of the white- and pink-hued boughs. There was a crisp breeze blowing through the trees. It was a vision of peace and tranquility.

Elizabeth stood there for a moment, and simply gazed at him.

No one could deny that Mr. Darcy was an exceedingly handsome man. And standing where she was, she could almost feel her heart softening at the sight.

That was... until she remembered his odious behavior in Meryton and what he had said about her on their very first meeting. A familiar grimace replaced the smile she had not realized had appeared on her lips. Elizabeth straightened her shoulders and approached him.

"Hello, Mr. Darcy!" she called, as she neared. "How are you doing on this fine day?"

The man seemed to jolt into awareness at her voice.

He turned, fixing her with a gaze of such intensity that she took an unconscious step back.

"Miss Elizabeth," he said. Then he peered at her in confusion.

"I am visiting Mr. Collins and his wife at the parsonage," she offered helpfully. "You may know the new Mrs. Collins as Charlotte Lucas from when you were last in Meryton."

Mr. Darcy did not reply.

When the silence became awkward and he continued to stare at her oddly, Elizabeth asked, "Did you only just arrive at Rosings?"

The confused look on Mr. Darcy's face intensified.

"Rosings?"

Elizabeth tipped her head to one side. She did not believe she had ever been in an interaction as strange as the one she was in right then.

"Yes. We had tea there yesterday." A frown touched her brows.

"Perhaps you heard about it from your aunt?"

Mr. Darcy's unceasing stare was beginning to disconcert her. Elizabeth felt a strange coldness *tip-tap* down her spine. She took another step back.

"Right, well... I shall leave you to it," she said. She gestured at the blooming cherry trees around them. "Good day, Mr. Darcy!"

She practically fled the scene.

Chapter 3:

THROUGH...AND THROUGH

S he saw him under the cherry trees the next day as well. Elizabeth huffed in annoyance.

Why could not Mr. Darcy choose a different path?

She wanted to enjoy the cherry blossoms while they lasted... which would be barely another week or so. She sighed.

As Lady Catherine's nephew, she supposed Mr. Darcy had a greater claim to the enjoyment of the cherry trees on the vast grounds of Rosings Park. Yet, once she returned to the parsonage, Elizabeth could not help but comment on the annoyance to Charlotte.

The conversation unfolded over tea in the small room at the back of the cottage.

"Mr. Darcy?" Charlotte asked, confusion evident on her face. "But Eliza, surely Mr. Collins would have mentioned something if Mr. Darcy was visiting."

Elizabeth frowned.

"Yes, I found that odd too."

She sipped her tea.

"Perhaps he was told not to?" she hedged. "Though I cannot imagine why."

"Hmm."

The two friends soon moved to other subjects of conversation.

The next day, Elizabeth decided to let go of her favourite walk and choose a new one.

As she saw it, there was no need to make much ado about the matter. Though, she was still stung over missing out on the fleeting pleasure of the cherry blossoms. But what was one to do?

So Elizabeth meandered through elm-lined paths, and past avenues bordered with black poplars and oaks, before finding herself in a small chestnut copse that seemed to have been left to grow untamed. Perhaps because there was no carriage path to it.

Elizabeth sighed happily as she spotted an iron bench and sank into it. Then, she closed her eyes, letting the gentle sunlight streaming through the gaps between the branches fall upon her upturned face.

The scent of early spring washed over her. So did the chirping of songbirds among the leaves.

It was both glorious and meditative.

"Miss Bennet?"

Elizabeth gasped, eyes flying open.

"Mr. Darcy!"

They stared at each other in shock.

...though why *he* should appear so was a mystery to her. *Was he not the one who sought her?*

Elizabeth looked about them. They were the only two in the copse.

"I was enjoying the trees," she said, getting to her feet even as a disconcerting feeling settled in her bones.

Mr. Darcy did not respond. Only continued to stare at her in that odd way. Elizabeth could feel the hair at the back of her neck prickle. He was wearing the same clothes as the ones she had seen him in yesterday.

...or was it the day before?

"I shall be on my way."

Elizabeth side-stepped the seemingly frozen man, wondering if it would be odd if she broke into a run. But she stifled the impulse and took a few more steps away, putting her back to Mr. Darcy.

"Miss Bennet, why do I see you?"

She paused.

Then she looked over her shoulder at him. "I do not understand your meaning, Mr. Darcy."

"Why *you*?"

She frowned. But he did not elaborate. She was now half turned towards him, and half away.

"Are you feeling well, sir?" she asked. She gestured at the iron bench, taking another step away from him. "Perhaps you should sit."

"Why do I see you, Miss Bennet!!?"

Mr. Darcy suddenly exploded. Elizabeth gasped in alarm. There was harsh anger on his face and a dark glare in his eyes.

"Sir! I would implore you to not speak to me in such a fashion!" she snapped.

She briskly walked towards the dirt path that led out of the copse, leaves crunching under her boots as she tried not to run. Alarm was ringing through her bones. Blood rushing past her ears.

"Miss Bennet, wait!"

Elizabeth gasped again. Fear thundered through her. She started to run. Mr. Darcy had sounded awfully close somewhere behind her, but she did not turn to look. She did not want to.

"Miss Bennet!"

"Desist sir!" she shouted, picking up her pace and tossing propriety to the wayside.

Her heart hammered within her chest. Trees rushed past her. She could not hear Mr. Darcy pursuing her anymore but she did not dare look back. Or stop.

"Miss Bennet..."

Elizabeth screamed as Mr. Darcy suddenly appeared before her. *As if out of thin air!*

But, by then, they were already set on a collision course. And she bludgeoned right into him...

...and straight out through the other side!

An intense chill overtook Elizabeth.

She faltered, and stopped. Almost as if someone had submerged her in ice cold water.

She turned. Breathless.

Mr. Darcy was staring at her with horror in his eyes. Then, he stared at his front where she had passed right through him.

"Good lord!" He patted his coat. "What was that?!"

Their eyes met. Realization dawned on her.

"Mr Darcy..." Elizabeth whispered, eyes widening.

But before she could say anything else...

...he disappeared.

Chapter 4:

LADY CATHERINE'S LAMENTS

"What is the matter, Eliza? You are frightening me!"

Charlotte wrapped another blanket around Elizabeth as she sat close to the fireplace with her teeth chattering uncontrollably.

Tremors shook her frame. She squeezed her eyes shut.

"Eliza, if you do not tell me what has happened, I shall have to fetch the apothecary!"

"Please... don... do not, Char..lotte," Elizabeth gritted out.

"At least drink your tea!"

Charlotte handed her the steaming cup after stirring three heaping spoonfuls of sugar in it. Elizabeth grimaced but sipped the tea nonetheless. And then she sipped some more as she immediately felt better. By the time she had drained the cup, her tremors had reduced dramatically.

"Let me make you another one," Charlotte said, taking the empty cup from her. But then she suddenly wrapped her fingers around Elizabeth's. "You are still freezing!"

Elizabeth grimaced as another tremor shot up her spine. She was thankful for the warmth of Charlotte's hands though.

"Charlotte, I think something is wrong with Mr. Darcy..." she whispered after her friend handed her a second cup of steaming sweet tea.

"Mr. Darcy?" Charlotte frowned. "What do you–"

"Charlotte! Charlotte!"

Loud calls could be heard from the front of the house. Mr. Collins had returned from his daily pilgrimage to Rosings. Charlotte sighed.

"I shall return soon," she said and stepped out of Elizabeth's room.

Elizabeth shivered and hugged the blankets closer to her. She could hear footsteps pounding up the stairs. And then Mr. Collins' loud voice echoed in the corridor beyond the door:

"There you are, Charlotte! We must make haste and attend to Lady Catherine!" he wheezed. "They have received terrible news!"

"Goodness, Mr. Collins! You are frightening me! What has happened?!" Charlotte's softer voice reached Elizabeth through the ajar door.

"It is Mr. Darcy!" Mr. Collins wailed. And then he coughed breathlessly. "His carriage..."

Another pause. A loud fit of coughs.

"...it has met with a terrible accident!"

Elizabeth gasped.

Later that evening...

Elizabeth did not know what was worse.

Seeing an apparition that resembled Mr. Darcy, or hearing of a carriage accident involving the gentleman while Lady Catherine made it all about herself.

"Four days they have kept him in that inn in the middle of nowhere!" Lady Catherine lamented.

All of them were sitting in Rosings' west parlour. Gloom written on every face.

"Four days, Mr. Collins! When his family is in easy distance."

Their tea lay unattended before them.

"I told Richard to bring him here," Lady Catherine continued. "But he refuses to listen to reason! I have been treated most heinously by my nephews and the Earl!"

Mr. Collins cooed affirmations and support even as Lady Catherine continued to lambast the decision of her relatives.

"Richard should have come to me as soon as the accident occurred! Instead, he went to London. *London!* When we are barely fifteen miles from Dunhill-on-Grom!"

Jenkinson—who was Miss de Bourgh's companion—shifted uncomfortably beside her charge. Elizabeth saw the woman's fingers twitch in her lap as her eyes flickered to the drooping shawl on Miss de Bourgh's shoulders.

"I am certain that Mr. Hanson would have attended to Fitzwilliam most diligently," Lady Catherine said. "Anne has never had any complaints under his care, and look how well she looks..."

Miss de Bourgh turned her face briefly towards the fireplace. The wanness of her complexion suddenly became stark for a moment.

"...and now Richard says Darcy cannot be moved until he heals! How my poor sister must be turning in her grave to think her darling son is festering in whichever hole they have contrived to situate him in."

"It is most badly done indeed," Mr. Collins agreed.

Elizabeth glanced at Charlotte. Her friend was staring longingly at the teapot on the table.

"I shall tell you, Mr. Collins," Lady Catherine continued. "I was of a mind to have Darcy removed to Rosings. But Richard refuses to disclose the directions. *Utterly refuses!* Darcy's own aunt. His mother's dearest sister! I have been most heinously treated by my relations!"

"Most heinously indeed," Mr. Collins echoed, shaking his head in sympathy.

Jenkinson shifted in her seat again. Miss de Bourgh's shawl was truly drooping on one side now. Elizabeth bit her lip.

"But you shall see, Mr. Collins. I shall prevail. I always have my way!" Lady Catherine fumed, striking the carpeted floor with her wooden staff.

The sound jolted everyone in the room to sit straighter. And Jenkinson hurried out of her seat to fix Miss de Bourgh's shawls. It seemed to stir fresh resentment in the occupants of the parlour.

Elizabeth stifled a sigh.

Chapter 5:

BLINK

It was three days since her encounter with Mr. Darcy's apparition. Elizabeth was not certain if what she had experienced was a dream or real.

Perhaps she had fallen asleep on that iron bench in that chestnut copse. Perhaps it had been nothing but her overactive imagination.

Yet, she had not gone for her usual walk since that day. Not since the news.

A shiver crept up Elizabeth's spine at the thought. She shook it off as best as she could and went back to tossing feed to the Collins' chickens.

"Are you real?"

Elizabeth screamed—nearly jumping out of her skin!—and dropped the bowl of feed. Mr. Darcy was standing a few feet away from her.

"Mr. Darcy..." she said in a hush. Eyes wide in horror.

"Why do I see you, Miss Bennet?" he asked, voice soft and melancholic.

It was almost as if he was speaking to himself, not her. Elizabeth could only stare at the man.

Her heart thumped loudly within her chest. Blood thundered past her ears, and within her veins. He was still dressed in the same clothes as the day she had spoken to him under the cherry trees.

She squeezed her eyes shut. And then opened them after a few moments. He was still there.

"Are you... real?" Elizabeth whispered.

Her hands were trembling. She closed her fingers in a fist to stop the shivers.

"Why do I see you, Miss Bennet?" Mr. Darcy asked, instead. Again. A forlorn note in his voice.

Their eyes met.

"How is this *possible*?" Elizabeth whispered.

There was a faintness to Mr. Darcy's outline in the sunlight that she had not noticed before. They looked at each other for a long moment. Silence stretched between them, even with the chicken clucking nearby.

"I keep looking for others," Mr. Darcy said. "But I only find you..."

His voice wrapped around her. Too intimately for her liking. Elizabeth steeled herself, drawing herself straight. A frown etched itself between her brows.

"Mr. Darcy, I do not know what you mean, but I would appreciate it if you would desist from haunting me!"

His eyes widened then, piercing her with his full attention.

"Haunting you?"

Elizabeth looked to the grass near her feet. The hens were clustered around the fallen seeds, busy pecking. *How did one go about breaking the news of a death to the very person in question?*

Elizabeth felt her heart squeeze. No matter her dislike for the man, she had to do it. She looked up, face paling.

"Mr. Darcy... sir... what do you remember?"

He tilted his head to one side.

"Remember?"

"Yes." Her cheeks coloured. "What was the last thing you remember... before your... current predicament?"

"My predicament?" He frowned. "I do not understand."

Elizabeth bit her lip.

"You said you keep looking for others but you can not find them."

She felt as if she was bumbling about like a donkey in a barn, but she hoped she would get wherever the conversation needed to go... eventually.

Why did she have to do this task?! Could not have Mr. Darcy chosen to haunt someone else?

Lady Catherine perhaps?

A distant look appeared in Mr. Darcy's eyes.

"I was in my carriage with Fitzwilliam," he said. His brows furrowed. "We had crossed the Dunhill bridge... and there was a... rapidly approaching carriage opposite us..."

Mr. Darcy's eyes widened. His eyes focused on Elizabeth again.

"There was a loud snap and..." Shock swept across his face. He stared.

"...my God!"

Elizabeth gasped as Mr. Darcy disappeared again.

Chapter 6:

ELIZABETH'S DILEMMA

"I do not know what the matter is with you, Eliza!"

Charlotte sat on the edge of the bed and touched Elizabeth's forehead. The latter moaned and burrowed under the covers as chills swept through her.

"I do not know..." she said, shivering.

Charlotte tsked and poured a generous cup of sweet tea for her. Then she blew on the steam curling over the rim. "Here, drink this."

Elizabeth accepted the offering, her freezing fingers eagerly wrapping around the warm porcelain. She sighed.

"Charlotte... I think I am losing my mind."

She took a sip. Once again, the sugar did its trick almost instantly.

"What nonsense! If I can tolerate Mr. Collins' quirks and keep my wits, surely you cannot be any worse for wear after only a few days."

Elizabeth gaped at her friend in surprise.

Then, a startled laugh bubbled out of her.

"I'm afraid, Mrs. Collins, that your husband is *not* to blame for my lack of wit."

Charlotte brushed a stray lock of hair behind her ear. "Then pray, tell me, what is the matter?" she asked gently.

Her eyes searched Elizabeth's face.

"I am afraid something has befallen you, Eliza, and you do not wish to tell me."

Tears pricked Elizabeth's eyes. She tried to blink them away, fixing her gaze on a stray thread on the covers over her knees. Her fingers were beginning to feel cold again, despite the steaming cup in her hands.

"I am afraid you will not believe me."

Another shudder swept through her as she remembered the sudden appearance and disappearance of a certain apparition. Elizabeth finished the rest of the tea in a single gulp.

Charlotte tsked again, taking the empty cup from her hands.

"You will be surprised at what I think is believable and unbelievable after seven-and-twenty years of life." She poured more tea into the cup. "Truly, will you not tell me?" She fixed a steady gaze on Elizabeth.

Elizabeth huffed. "I know all your tricks, Charlotte. We have been friends for too long."

"Then, tell me, does it have something to do with Mr. Darcy?"

Elizabeth gasped. Charlotte gave her a rueful smile.

"I remember you were telling me something about him, the last time you were like this. Before we were interrupted." Charlotte added two more heaping spoonfuls of sugar to the fresh cup of tea and stirred it.

Elizabeth closed her eyes for a moment.

"You are not wrong. But in this instance, you will have to trust me, Charlotte." She accepted the offered tea.

"I wish to resolve this matter on my own."

Chapter 7:

NIGHT VISITOR

T he next time she saw Mr. Darcy, Elizabeth was *not* prepared. (Despite telling herself she would be.)

But then again, she had not expected to wake up with a fright and find him sitting on the chair beside her bed!

"Goodness gracious!"

Elizabeth clutched at the covers tightly and stared at Mr. Darcy. He appeared the same as before. Handsome. Well-coiffed. Dressed in his great coat and fawn pants, with a white silk cravat around his neck.

"I apologize, Miss Bennet, for scaring you," Mr. Darcy said, almost regretfully. "I could not help myself."

A flash of annoyance speared through Elizabeth.

Of all the ghosts that could have haunted her, it was the man she detested the most! Her fear disappeared at the heels of her anger.

"What do you want, Mr. Darcy?" she asked coldly.

He paled. And then cleared his throat.

"It is not what I want. It is what I... find myself in," he said. His gaze fixed on her in the dun darkness. "Am I dead, Miss Bennet? Is that why..." He fell silent and stared at his hands resting on the arms of the chair.

A pang of sorrow touched Elizabeth's heart. She bit her lip. No matter her personal dislike of the man, she would not have wished death upon him.

"I believe so. But I do not know..." she said after a moment.

A sudden lump formed in her throat.

She could not imagine a world without Jane in it. Or her beloved father. She wondered about Mr. Darcy's sister, and the cousin he had been with when the carriage overturned.

"News of your... demise... has not reached Rosings. I am sorry," she whispered.

A tear rolled down her face, startling her. Mr. Darcy looked startled too. Then he smiled sadly.

"It was not your fault."

Elizabeth shook her head and sat up, carefully drawing the covers up with her, so she could rest against the headboard.

"Your cousin, Colonel Fitzwilliam, sent news to Rosings," she said. "The services of a physician from town has been engaged and Lord Matlock has you ensconced somewhere in the Kent countryside. They are hopeful you will heal."

She paused.

"...at least, that was what was conveyed."

"Then why am I here?" Mr. Darcy asked her.

They were silent for a moment.

"I must be close to death if nothing else," he added, and then sighed, looking towards the window. "Perhaps Lord Matlock does not want news of my death getting out. Though, I cannot imagine why."

Elizabeth watched Mr. Darcy shift on the chair. There was a certain restlessness in his form. It was strange to have him in her room while she was in her bedclothes under the covers. A deep blush erupted over her cheeks.

"How are you sitting on that chair?" Elizabeth asked abruptly.

Mr. Darcy looked at her in surprise. Then he looked at his hands on the chair arms. Almost as if he had not thought of that at all.

"I... am not certain."

Elizabeth sat forward, careful to cling to the covers. "That day in that copse... when I ran into you..." Her face heated some more. "Did you..."

She cleared her throat.

"Did you... feel something when I...?"

Mr. Darcy looked just as embarrassed as her. He stared at her covers.

"You mean the day you...?" He appeared to be blushing, but Elizabeth could not be certain. "Uh... I did not."

Elizabeth looked down at her covers. "Well, right then."

She could feel the flush spreading right down to her toes. She clutched at the covers more tightly. Mr. Darcy cleared his throat.

"I can walk through doors, in case you were wondering."

Elizabeth looked up in surprise. And curiosity. Then she tipped her head to one side.

"That must be strange."

He smiled, still embarrassed. "Yes."

"And you truly cannot see..." She could feel her face heating again. "...anyone else but me?"

Mr. Darcy shook his head.

"Only you."

A frisson of something unknowable passed through Elizabeth. Mr. Darcy's gaze locked on her, and held. Then he looked away.

"I can hardly imagine what that must be like," she said, softly.

To be the only one in a land of empty houses and empty streets. To not hear a single voice. And the only person one could see was... Miss Bingley?

Elizabeth shuddered immediately.

Of course, she was not Miss Bingley! But she reckoned it must be something like so for Mr. Darcy. After all, he found her barely tolerable.

"I apologize for inconveniencing you and breaking propriety, Miss Bennet..."

Her attention was drawn back to Mr. Darcy.

"...but I do not know how to stop this."

Their gazes locked on each other once more. This time he had a distinct look of despondency about him. She could feel it too. Elizabeth bit her lip.

"Can you not go anywhere at all?" she asked.

He was silent for a moment. And then he shook his head.

"I tried walking out of Hunsford one time. But the next thing I remember was standing beside you in that copse of chestnuts."

Elizabeth hugged the covers closer to herself.

They were silent for a moment longer.

Each lost in their own thoughts.

"Why do you think you are here?" Her voice was a hush in the silence.

"I do not know."

He looked to the windows again. A deep sorrow was etched on his face.

"...maybe all this is just a dream and I will wake up tomorrow."

Elizabeth could feel her eyes prickling. But she did not want to think about death and dying any longer. She tried to shake it off.

"Well, Mr. Darcy, I hope you are right."

She tried to strike some cheerfulness, but was certain she was failing. He looked her way.

"...but if you are not, might you find a better time to haunt me?"

Mr. Darcy looked embarrassed again.

"I will try my best, Miss Bennet."

Chapter 8:

AFTERNOON BREEZE

E lizabeth was better prepared the next time she saw Mr. Darcy. But barely so.

"Goodness!" She yelped when he appeared beside her on the garden bench the very next afternoon. Then she har-rumphed in indignation as she looked at him.

"I apologize for startling you, Miss Bennet." The tips of his ears were turning red. Elizabeth wondered at that. But then sighed.

"Well, I suppose, you cannot help it."

It was a lazy afternoon with the sun slanting across the west side of the parsonage, illuminating the dun brick walls and wooden window frames. Charlotte's peony bushes looked ex-ceptionally beautiful in the light. As did Mr. Collins' vegetable garden a little further away.

Elizabeth had come outside to sit on the bench in the shade and read a book. Well... she could hardly read now. Not with Mr. Darcy sitting beside her. She shut the book with a snap.

"The dream persists," she said, turning her full attention to him.

He gave her a wry smile. "Unfortunately."

They were silent for a moment.

"Have you wondered why you are... the way you are?" Elizabeth could feel her cheeks heating as she fixed her gaze on his face.

The slight translucency of his features against the sunlight was not enough to hide the handsomeness of his features. His dark, expressive eyes. The slightly arrogant, roman nose. The sharp line of his jaws with the perfectly groomed sideburns. Elizabeth looked away quickly.

"I do not know," Mr. Darcy said.

"Perhaps you have some unfinished business?" she hedged.

"I cannot imagine what that might be."

"Well, since you are at Rosings..." she said. "Might it have something to do with Lady Catherine?"

Mr. Darcy visibly grimaced. "I do not think so."

"How about your cousin? Miss de Bourgh," she asked. "I heard you were to marry her."

He shook his head. An annoyed flush appeared on his face. "That is a figment of my aunt's imagination." Then he sighed. "It does not explain why I can only see you."

Their eyes met and held.

Elizabeth could feel her cheeks heating even more. She cleared her throat and stared at the book in her hand. The two of them were silent for the longest time, with only the sound of rustling leaves and the occasional chirp of an afternoon bird.

"What if I wrote a letter to your cousin?" she asked suddenly.

Mr. Darcy looked surprised. "My cousin?"

"I meant Colonel Fitzwilliam. We could find out what happened to you."

He was silent for a moment longer.

And then he fixed his gaze on her again. There was a deep sadness in them.

"I am willing to try anything," he said softly.

Elizabeth felt her heart twist in her chest.

"And perhaps, once we find out..." Mr. Darcy continued. "I would be much obliged to you, Miss Bennet, if you could write a letter to my sister for me."

Chapter 9:

AN OVERBEARANCE OF INDISCRETION

"Not like that, Jenkinson!" Lady Catherine snapped. "You know how I detest sloppiness!"

The poor woman's hands trembled violently, and the tea she was pouring out splashed everywhere on the tray. Elizabeth stifled a sigh.

"Oh, for heaven's sake!"

Jenkinson placed the pot back on the table, her face paling. "I apologize for my clumsiness, your ladyship!" She had begun to wring her hands almost compulsively.

Elizabeth eyed Miss de Bourgh. The latter had her face angled away from the scene, staring almost in a trance-like fashion at the woodfire in the grate.

"It is so hard to find competent help these days..." Lady Catherine continued, shooing away Jenkinson with a wave of her hand.

The woman practically ran to pull at the servant's bell.

"...I despair, Mr. Collins!"

"Quite right," Mr. Collins said, ever eager to please his patroness.

Maria Lucas shifted uncomfortably in her seat next to Elizabeth.

The party from the parsonage had been summoned that evening to keep Lady Catherine company. No matter that Charlotte already had dinner plans in place and had asked Mrs. Bishop to have the leg of mutton prepared that day.

"Has there been any improvement in Mr. Darcy's condition?"

Everyone looked at Elizabeth.

But she kept her eyes on Lady Catherine. A deep frown appeared on the older lady's face.

"Richard has not seen fit to keep me abreast of any more news," Lady Catherine said. Disgruntlement was clear in the tone of her voice.

Then her gaze sharpened on Elizabeth like a hawk.

"I hope you are not so unfilial towards your own family, Miss Bennet," she said. She narrowed her eyes. "I know there was a certain matter of a wedding that *did not* take place."

Elizabeth kept her expression neutral, though she could see Charlotte turn pink with embarrassment on her other side. Mr. Collins was looking her way, too, with keen scrutiny.

"I hope I am as filial as is within my capacity," Elizabeth said. "As for the wedding, the matter was resolved in a far more satisfactory manner, in my opinion. I doubt anyone can find fault there."

"Indeed," Lady Catherine said, narrowing her eyes some more. "You are five sisters, are you not? And all unmarried?"

"Yes, your ladyship."

"And your father's estate is entailed away to Mr. Collins."

It was not a question.

"That is correct, your ladyship!" Mr. Collins said when Elizabeth did not answer immediately.

Lady Catherine glared at him for interrupting. He grew red as a beet and settled back in his chair.

"Well, Miss Bennet, providence shall bring what is in one's destiny."

Then she looked at her daughter and sighed.

"I had hoped Fitzwilliam would marry Anne this year. He has had enough years gallivanting as a bachelor."

Elizabeth barely held back her eyebrows from rising up her forehead. "Gallivanting" was *not* a word one could use for Mr. Darcy. "Dreadful" perhaps. Maybe even "haughty". Though, she had to admit that his ghostly self was not half as dreadful as he had been in Meryton some months prior.

They were interrupted as a maid entered the parlour to clear away the spilled tea tray. A fresh one was brought in soon after.

Jenkinson quickly took up her place by the table once more. Face fixed in concentration—and a little fear.

"Yes, I believe they would have married this year," Lady Catherine continued. "If only the wretched accident had not taken place!"

She stamped her wooden staff on the carpet as she was wont to do. Jenkinson almost spilled the tea once more. Maria Lucas gasped...and then tried to cover it with a small cough.

"If only Richard would tell me Fitzwilliam's whereabouts! We might conduct the nuptials before it is too late."

Chapter 10:

CHANGED HEART...OR PERHAPS NOT

The cherry trees were in full bloom when Elizabeth walked on her favourite path the next day. She sighed happily.

Pale white and blush pink petals were drifting down from the boughs above her. Their soft perfume wafted in the air. She extended a hand and caught a stray bloom in her palm.

"Miss Bennet."

Elizabeth yelped and clutched at her front, flower petal crushed in a fist. Her heart hammered wildly.

"Mr. Darcy! You really must stop doing that!"

He looked embarrassed.

"I apologize for interrupting you."

Elizabeth straightened her straw hat and sighed.

"It is no matter."

They were silent for a moment, even as the wind blew her curls around her face and did not stir a single strand of his.

"Would you like to join me?" she asked at last. "I was enjoying the trees in this part of the avenue. I am quite partial to them."

"Yes," he said, a relieved smile on his face.

They fell into step.

Morning sunlight shone down on them through the lattice of branches and leaves.

"I was thinking about what I might write to your cousin," Elizabeth said after a while.

Mr. Darcy did not say anything. So she continued.

"I do not know if I should mention... your current predicament. Would the Colonel take kindly to a letter from a practical stranger?"

"No, he would not," Mr. Darcy said.

"Hmm."

The path curved away from the imposing view of Rosings house.

"Perhaps I can..."

"I apologize for cutting in, Miss Bennet, but I am not certain if you should write to Richard at all," Mr. Darcy said.

Elizabeth glanced at him curiously.

"You wished to yesterday. Did you change your mind?"

"Yes."

Mr. Darcy pinked visibly. "I do not want him to have the wrong impression of you."

Elizabeth kept her eyes fixed on the cherry trees ahead of them, though her face warmed. She fiddled with her gloves. It would be rather inconvenient if anyone were to believe she and Mr. Darcy had some scandalous relations between them. She bit her lip.

"Well, I do not know how else we might find out anything. Colonel Fitzwilliam has not been very forthcoming with Lady Catherine, to her eternal displeasure."

They walked in silence for a while, with only the sound of her walking shoes crunching gravel underfoot.

Then Elizabeth suddenly looked up. "Oh, how could I forget?!"

It was Mr. Darcy's turn to look curiously at her.

"Lady Catherine summoned us for dinner yesterday," she said. "She wants to find out where you are convalescing, so she may marry Miss de Bourgh to you."

Instant alarm shot across Mr. Darcy's face.

"Absolutely not!"

Elizabeth smiled wryly at his reaction.

"I believe you are quite safe from such machinations. As I said earlier, Lady Catherine is not very happy with your cousin's lack of forthcomingness."

"Good," Mr. Darcy said, looking relieved. But then he grew contemplative.

They continued to walk.

"Miss Bennet, I think a letter to Richard cannot be avoided."

"Hmm?"

The breeze had slowed but birdsong was still heavy in the air. Elizabeth looked at the cherry blossoms drifting around them. "How do you propose we prevent any... er, wrong impressions?"

Mr. Darcy stopped walking. She did too.

"You must tell him about me."

Their gazes locked on one another.

"Do you mean...?"

"Yes."

"Hmm."

Elizabeth wondered how *that* would be regarded. It was not everyday that one received a letter about the ghost of one's cousin!

Chapter 11:

NIGHT VISITOR, DEUX

Elizabeth was prepared when she saw Mr. Darcy next.

Unfortunately, it was not where she had hoped to meet him again. She sighed.

"Mr. Darcy."

His outline was less distinct in the darkness of her room. The moon had begun to wane and there were clouds in the night sky.

"I truly did not intend to importune you this way…" he said. She could hear the strain in his voice.

"It is no matter," Elizabeth said, moving the covers aside and getting out of her bed. She was still dressed in her dinner clothes. "As you can see, I anticipated something like this would happen."

An embarrassed silence stretched between them. Elizabeth bit her lip as a stray thought came to her.

"I was wondering if you have ever manifested... in this state..." she gestured at him. "When I was not aware."

The silence seemed to thicken, growing more uncomfortable. She could feel the back of her neck heating. But she persisted.

"Mr. Darcy, if your appearances are somewhat like clockwork, I believe it is something we must consider," she said, growing exasperated at his continued silence. "Perhaps your cousin can shed some light on it if I were to mention it in the letter."

"I... had not considered that," Mr. Darcy said at last. He shifted where he stood.

Elizabeth lit the candle on the table beside her bed. Dull warm light suffused the area around them. She looked at Mr. Darcy. He still looked embarrassed.

"Let me arrange the writing desk, then we may begin."

"You wish to write the letter now?" he asked as she moved past him with the candle.

"Well, to be honest," she glanced at him. "I would prefer to sleep. But since you are here, I do not see why not."

"I apologize–"

"It is no matter," Elizabeth said again, quickly, before matters got any more awkward.

She pointed to the other chair in her room that she had set up beside the writing desk just for this. "You may sit here if you please."

Mr. Darcy shifted uncomfortably once more. He did not seem to know what to do with his hands. Elizabeth looked away, settling herself in her own chair.

Moments later, once Mr. Darcy was in the chair she had offered him, and she was arranging paper and ink, he spoke unexpectedly.

"I usually find myself here—in Hunsford, I mean—in the mornings or afternoons."

Elizabeth paused.

"I cannot discern a pattern in that regard."

Their eyes met.

"I try to look for a stray post, or a newspaper, to get my bearings," he added.

Elizabeth settled back in her chair, letting go of the papers in her hand.

"...but I am always here in the evenings," Mr. Darcy said. He seemed to go red at that.

"I try to wander about the house. I can walk through doors... as you know."

He trailed off. The silence grew awkward between them once more.

Elizabeth shifted in her seat even as her cheeks flamed. She was not certain what perturbed her more. The thought of Mr. Darcy watching her while she was asleep. Or sharing such an unexpected—and frankly disconcerting—intimacy with the last man she would wish to share such a thing with.

She bit her lip. "Well... should we begin?"

"Yes," Mr. Darcy said, hurriedly.

But Elizabeth paused once more.

"Mr. Darcy...?" She looked at him. "I wonder how you change colour." She grew a tad red in the face. "I meant, when you are embarrassed. Should not ghostly presences have... er, a fixed visage?"

His eyebrows climbed up his forehead.

"I did not know I did that."

"Oh."

Then Elizabeth glanced at the mirror in the room.

"Have you, perchance, tried to glimpse at your reflection?"

"Yes..." he said, looking embarrassed once more. "I... could not see one."

Elizabeth looked at him, shocked. "Truly?"

"Yes."

"Hmm..."

"What are you thinking?" he asked when Elizabeth was silent for a while, glancing between him and the mirror.

"Well, it is only a curiosity..." she said. "Would you care to stand beside me in front of the mirror? I was wondering if I might see you."

A relieved smile flashed across Mr. Darcy's face. He stood up. But Elizabeth found herself staring at him. The man was truly was handsome when he did not look sour, or vexed at the world.

"Miss Bennet?"

She blinked and looked away. Then got to her feet.

Chapter 12:

Tea with Charlotte

They were not able to get to the letter that night. Not from lack of trying, though.

It was the oddest thing.

One moment, Elizabeth was standing next to Mr. Darcy in front of the mirror, staring at the astonishing fact that she *too* could not see him in the mirror. And the next—she had turned her face towards him, catching his eyes, surprised at how close they were...

...when he abruptly disappeared.

Elizabeth had looked about the room, unsure if he was truly gone. But Mr. Darcy was nowhere to be found.

So she had waited for him to appear for another hour before sleep had claimed her naturally.

Elizabeth did the next best thing when she woke up the morning—she stuffed some loose pages and a pencil in her reticule and took it with her on her morning ramble.

But Mr. Darcy did not show up anywhere.

Not in the avenue of cherry trees.

Or in the chestnut copse.

Or anywhere else.

Feeling defeated, Elizabeth finally returned to the parsonage after some hours. And there she almost collided with Maria Lucas on her way inside.

"Goodness, Lizzy! Will you watch where you are going?"

"Oh!"

Elizabeth clutched a hand to her chest.

"Maria! Is that Eliza?" Charlotte's voice rang out from within the morning parlour.

"Yes, it is!" Maria answered back. And then she stepped around Elizabeth. "Who were you talking to yesterday night?"

Elizabeth froze, and then quickly fixed a quizzical look on the girl. "Talking?"

"Yes," Maria said, a small frown appearing on her lips. "I heard you speaking to someone for quite a while. I thought it was Charlotte, but she said it was not."

"Oh..."

"Eliza! Can you come in here for a moment before you go upstairs?" Charlotte's voice rang out again from the parlour.

"Yes!" she called back. Then she looked at Maria. "I do not know what you mean. Perhaps you were dreaming."

Maria raised an eyebrow that reminded Elizabeth of her second-youngest sister, Kitty, before she walked out of the gate. Elizabeth shrugged and entered the parlour.

"There you are, Eliza," Charlotte said, smiling at her. "Would you like to have some tea?"

"Yes, that would be lovely," she said, setting her reticule aside before taking a seat near the windows.

The day was coming along quite pleasantly with warm sunlight painting the view outside a soft pastel green. Charlotte settled down beside her.

"Did you enjoy your walk?"

Elizabeth took the teacup from her friend with a smile.

"Yes, I did. Though I apologize for missing breakfast. The paths here are so beautiful, I could not bear coming back any sooner."

Charlotte smiled at her and then sipped her tea.

"I am glad to hear that. I was worried you would find our life in Hunsford unvaried and dull."

"Not at all, my dear Charlotte," Elizabeth said, and grinned. "If anything, I am glad to escape all three hours of Mary practising her piano every morning."

Charlotte laughed.

The two friends spoke of mundane things for a while and all the developments in Meryton since Charlotte's departure from her childhood home. All the things they had not had a chance to talk about until then. But soon, the conversation turned elsewhere.

"Well, Eliza, you must know I want to talk about what happened yesterday at Rosings."

Elizabeth raised her eyebrows. *Did she mean Lady Catherine's unrelenting verbal assault on everyone?*

"Of course."

"I do not wish there to be any ill feelings between us because of anything Lady Catherine may have said."

Elizabeth grimaced.

"Charlotte, there are no ill feelings between us. And I spoke truly. You have done the station of Mrs. Collins far more good than I ever could have. Everything here is so beautiful and well-managed."

"Oh Eliza, that is very kind of you to say!"

Charlotte drew her into an impulsive hug. Elizabeth hugged her back, surprised.

"I was worried you were offended by what Mr. Collins said yesterday at dinner," Charlotte continued once they pulled apart. "You do not usually stay outside for so long, so I was wondering if it was because you wished to avoid him."

An incredulous—and slightly strained—laugh burst out of Elizabeth. *If only they knew!*

"Dear Charlotte, forgive me for saying this about your husband, but you know how much I love absurdity. It would take a lot more than what Mr. Collins said yesterday for me to be offended by him."

Then she grew sober.

"I just hope Mr. Collins has not been giving you a hard time." She searched Charlotte's face. "I was more offended by how he and Lady Catherine were speaking of the circumstances around *his* marriage while you were right across the table!"

Charlotte rolled her eyes.

"Eliza, you know I am not a romantic. I wanted my own home and now I have one. And Mr. Collins is harmless."

She laughed seeing the skeptical look on Elizabeth's face.

"No, truly! I shall tell you my secret to a happy marriage," she added. "I just give Mr. Collins more things to talk about and nod my head whenever he looks my way."

Elizabeth burst out into true laughter, and then covered her mouth with a hand.

"Oh, Charlotte! I have to be honest with you," she said. "I was in despair since your wedding day. But now I shall set it aside and trust your superior wisdom."

"You must, Eliza, you absolutely must!" Charlotte said with a grin. Then she added, "And you may call Mr. Collins as absurd as you wish when it is just the two of us."

"I shall hold you to it."

Chapter 13:

SCOTS PINE

The next two days passed in a rather mundane way.

Mr. Darcy was still missing, which caused Elizabeth more concern than she had believed she would feel for the man. She even thought of penning the letter to Colonel Fitzwilliam all by herself... until she remembered that she did not have an address to send it to. And she was *not* going to ask Lady Catherine for it if she could help it.

But then, on the afternoon of the third day, when she decided to go read a book in the garden under the shade of the large Scots pine tree, Mr. Darcy suddenly appeared.

"Goodness, Mr. Darcy!" Elizabeth cried as her heart practically leapt out of her chest. "Someone should tie a bell to you!"

"I apolo–"

"Yes, yes, I know!" she said, standing up and dusting her skirts. She glared at him.

"Where were you? I thought something had happened!"

Elizabeth twisted her shaking fingers into her skirt as she took in his appearance. For the most part, Mr. Darcy looked the same as always. But there was a new gauntness to his face. She frowned. "Are you unwell?"

"I..." Mr. Darcy started. And then he simply stared at her.

A slow blush crept onto Elizabeth's face at the intensity in his gaze. As if he could read something that surprised him.

"...I do not know," he said.

"Where were you?" Elizabeth repeated more quietly. The *thump-thump-thump* in her chest had begun to slow down.

"I..." Mr. Darcy frowned and then looked around them. "Am I in the parsonage?"

She nodded.

He did not say anything for a moment. Just took in the trees and bushes, before his eyes settled on the book she had left at the foot of the pine, next to her reticule.

"I hope I am not interrupting you, Miss Bennet."

Elizabeth shook her head. She let go of her skirts and tried to strike an image of composure. Her fingers twinged as blood rushed back into them.

"It has been two days since I last saw you," she said. "I was... worried."

They stood silently across from each other. Their gazes locked. There was a softness in Mr. Darcy's eyes that Elizabeth had never seen before. And then she noticed the faint pink creeping across his face.

"I do not know where I was," he said. "The last thing I remember was standing next to you... in your room before the mirror."

Surprise lifted Elizabeth's eyebrows.

"Oh."

She quickly picked up her reticule from the ground. Then she partially pulled out the folded pages and pencil from within. "I have been carrying these with me in hopes you will appear." Her face heated suddenly. She bit her lip.

"Ah... sorry to keep you waiting," Mr. Darcy said.

They both shifted uncertainly, across from each other.

In another moment, they were both seated on the garden bench only a little distance away from the Scots pine.

"Well," Elizabeth said. She had her sheaf of pages in her lap, cushioned over her book. Pencil in hand. "I am ready when you are, Mr. Darcy."

They started to work on the letter.

At first, it was a simple enough task.

They had to make the letter urgent enough so Colonel Fitzwilliam would not ignore it, or set it aside. Elizabeth decided to do away with civilities while remaining formal. But soon they reached the point where she had to prove she was indeed communicating with Mr. Darcy's spirit.

"Gracious, Mr. Darcy! I would have never imagined you capable of this."

Elizabeth nearly snorted as she finished writing about the "Fitzwilliam secret stash" and how a young Darcy had kicked his older cousin into an overfilled ditch because of a dispute over jam and scones.

"I aim to please," he said, a satisfied smirk on his face.

Elizabeth stared at him for a moment. And then burst into laughter.

"A jest, Mr. Darcy? I would not have believed you capable of that either if I had not heard it myself."

Mr. Darcy smiled ruefully at her. "There is much about me you do not know, Miss Bennet."

"So it seems," Elizabeth said, sobering immediately.

He was not wrong.

She had only started to realize that.

Mr. Darcy looked at her questioningly, but she shook her head.

They continued with their task. And after a while Mr. Darcy requested that she finish the rest of the letter in his words. It would lend more authenticity... or so he said.

Elizabeth just hoped Colonel Fitzwilliam would believe it. She was risking much by writing to an unrelated man. That too about such an outlandish thing!

But it was only once they reached the part where Mr. Darcy began to speak of his sister...

—and Elizabeth had barely scratched out a line on the page—

...when he suddenly seemed to choke up, and vanished once more!

Chapter 14:

INCONVENIENT SUMMONS

"Eliza, are you feeling unwell?"

Elizabeth looked up, startled. Her eyes fixed on Charlotte. All the inhabitants of the parsonage were currently at the dinner table, enjoying a modest but elegant spread.

"I am well."

"You seem distracted, Cousin Elizabeth," Mr. Collins said, peering at her from his seat at the head of the table.

Elizabeth smiled blandly at him. She was in no mood to have him pry into her life.

"I was simply enjoying the wonderful dinner, Mr. Collins." She glanced at her plate. There was a cut of beef and seasoned potatoes on it. "The potatoes are... very good."

Mr. Collins puffed up with pride immediately and nodded.

"Lady Catherine personally recommended Mrs. Potts to me," he said. "And what a delight she has been to Charlotte and me! Did I tell you about..."

Elizabeth nodded at all the appropriate places as Mr. Collins went into a lengthy monologue about chefs and cooks named after kitchen utensils and ingredients, and how the chef at Rosings was a "Monsieur Barbeau" who was known for his smoked salmon and breakfast kippers. Much like "Mrs. Potts" who was known for her pot roasts. Lady Catherine—as it turned out—was quite fond of having servants with names that echoed the position they held.

But she stopped listening after a while. It was the third time Mr. Collins had told them that particular story about his kitchen staff.

Her mind was fixed, instead, on the second disappearance of Mr. Darcy. She was beginning to really worry...

Knock!

Knock!

Knock!

Elizabeth startled out of her reverie as loud sounds of knocking reached them in the dining room from the front of the house.

"Who might it be at this time!?!"

Mr. Collins got out of his chair with a grunt. A sour pucker on his lips. They could hear the door being unlatched downstairs.

"That must be Janet," Charlotte said, quickly following after her husband as he left the room.

Maria shared a glance with Elizabeth. Eyes wide.

"Do you think it is from Rosings?"

"I do not know," Elizabeth said, equally stunned.

Both of them hurried out of the room as well.

It was Lady Catherine.

...or rather, an urgent summons to Rosings.

"Her ladyship would like all of us to join her..." Mr. Collins said, reading the missive that had come from the great house. "For dinner!" He looked up, surprised, and handed the note to Charlotte.

"Something must have happened, Charlotte! I must dress at once! Lady Catherine has need of me."

In what Elizabeth could only describe as an alarming display of dexterity from a man of such plodding proportions, Mr. Collins was out of the corridor—and then the house—in under ten minutes. All while the women were still arranging for their unfinished dinner to be removed.

On his way out, though, Mr. Collins urged them—in what had to be the shrillest voice Elizabeth had ever heard from him—to hurry and not keep her ladyship waiting. She sighed.

"Are you truly well, Eliza?"

Charlotte stopped her with a hand on her arm as she was about to make her way to the stairs.

"You look rather pale. If you wish to stay back, I can tell her ladyship you have a megrim."

Elizabeth gave her friend a wane smile.

"I am well, Charlotte. Thank you for asking. But I would very much like to know what the urgent news is."

"As would I!" Maria announced, coming to a stop next to her sister. She had been at the window moments ago, watching Mr. Collins' departure. "I wonder if it has anything to do with Mr. Darcy."

Charlotte fixed a piercing look on Elizabeth. "Yes, I wonder the same."

Elizabeth kept her face as bland as she could.

"I believe we should dress if we do not wish to incur her ladyship's wrath."

"Yes," Maria said, unmindful of the sudden tension. "I hope the carriage is sent back. I do not want to walk that far."

The carriage was not sent back.

Elizabeth stared at the patterns on the Persian carpet where the hem of her dress lay haphazardly. The intricate red and brown floral design clashed ostentatiously with the light green cotton of her visiting dress. Too simple. Too plain. She sipped her tea.

"Mr. Collins, I am displeased! I am very displeased!"

Lady Catherine struck the carpeted floor on her side of the parlour with the blunt end of her walking staff.

Thump! Thump! Thump!

"I have the most ungrateful and undutiful nephews in all of England!"

Elizabeth looked up as Miss de Bourgh coughed from her usual seat near the fireplace. Jenkinson was scurrying around her—as was usual too—adjusting the enormous shawls wrapped around her petite frame. And then the woman adjusted the fire screen for the tenth time.

"I sympathize with your ladyship," Mr. Collins said, nodding emphatically. "It is life's greatest sorrows when one's kin disabuses one of the sanctity of house and home, and familial bonds."

Elizabeth eyed the fire screen next to Miss de Bourgh. It had an intricate pattern of mourning doves and sparrows, nestled in abundant foliage, with gilded flourishes everywhere. It was just as ostentatious as everything else in Rosings.

"Yes, yes, Mr. Collins," Lady Catherine said impatiently. "But I have not given up on my wishes. I will have my way!"

She thumped her staff on the carpet again, startling Jenkinson who had only just returned to her seat and was about to take a sip of tea. The cup rattled on the saucer for a moment before Jenkinson froze.

"I have sent my men to follow Richard's man in secret. I must discover where he has Darcy holed up," Lady Catherine continued.

She watched as Jenkinson almost sighed in relief and finally had some tea. Elizabeth wished to breathe out a deep sigh of frustration as well.

Ever since they had arrived at Rosings, it had become apparent to all what Lady Catherine's primary object had been behind sending the urgent summons.

She had received a rather flimsy missive from her other nephew—The Honourable Harold Fitzwilliam, first son and heir of the Earl of Matlock (Lady Catherine's younger brother)—which contained scarce news of Mr. Darcy's health and recovery, and nothing of actual import that the lady wished to know. She was livid.

"Your astuteness is admirable as always, your ladyship," Mr. Collins said.

Of course, Mr. Collins was ever eager to please his patroness. But Elizabeth wished the rest of them had not been drawn into her vortex of indignation.

"I shall have Anne ready in the carriage the minute I know where Darcy is!" Lady Catherine said. "You, of course, must come with us, Mr. Collins. I shall have you officiate the wedding."

"I am ever your humble servant," Mr. Collins said, bowing from his seat in the ridiculous manner he always did. It almost upset the cup in his hand.

Elizabeth almost gave in to her urge to sigh.

The news of Mr. Darcy had been insubstantial enough to both increase her worries over his sudden disappearance and also calm them. She was divided in her mind.

She only wished Lady Catherine would request dinner soon so they might—*she might!*—return to the parsonage.

Chapter 15:

ASTUTE

E lizabeth set the bowl of chicken feed down on the grass and watched the birds abandon their stray pecking to swarm the food. She stepped back.

She had tried to stay awake the previous night in hopes of having Mr. Darcy appear. Tried to occupy herself by copying the penciled letter out on fresh sheets with ink. But then she had given in to her drooping eyelids after a few hours.

Elizabeth sighed and wiped her hands on the sides of her skirt. She went inside.

"Eliza, there you are!"

She looked up just as Charlotte stepped off the staircase and smiled at her.

"Charlotte," she smiled back. "Did you need me?"

"Not precisely. But I would like your company for tea."

"Of course."

Once the tea things were arranged and they each had a cup in their possession, Charlotte eyed Elizabeth with more intensity than usual.

"What is it?" Elizabeth asked in exasperation. She knew that look.

"I was wondering what you made of the matter with Mr. Darcy."

"Mr. Darcy?" Elizabeth's eyebrows climbed up her forehead. She quickly sipped some tea.

"Poor man. I pray for his speedy recovery," Charlotte said, tsking in regret. "I know I should not be saying this, for it does not concern me or my family, but it does not sit right with me what Lady Catherine is attempting to do."

Elizabeth frowned. Lady Catherine's obsession *was* unsettling.

"I believe Mr. Darcy's cousins will prevent any interference," she said. "They have been very secretive so far."

Charlotte reached for a biscuit. "Yes, but I can see how there might be a wish for a marriage between Mr. Darcy and Miss de Bourgh. They both have their inheritances, which is significant as I hear from Mr. Collins, though I believe Pemberley is much larger than Rosings..."

Surprise raised Elizabeth's eyebrows higher.

Rosings was a very large estate, she knew. *How much larger was Pemberley?*

"...Lady Catherine has been vocal about joining the two houses. I believe she wishes to keep the wealth in the family..."

Was this the reason behind Mr. Darcy's prideful manner-isms and lofty conceit?

"...so I cannot imagine Lord Matlock being opposed to such a union..."

But then why was Mr. Darcy such a close friend to Mr. Bingley?

"...nevertheless, it does not sit right with me to have them marry the man while he is not in his senses..."

She knew of Lady Catherine's disdain for the trading class, which was not a different opinion from that of the other members of the peerage and gentility. And everyone in Meryton knew that Mr. Bingley's father had been a man of business, who had only sold his factories to raise his children as gentry, away from the touch of trade.

"...what do you think, Eliza?"

Besides, Mr. Darcy had not behaved badly with her or acted imperiously since she encountered his apparition. Not once.

"Eliza?"

And he had never broken propriety, other than the unavoid-*able, despite having the opportunity...*

"Elizabeth!"

She startled out of her thoughts—almost spilling the tea in her cup—when Charlotte gently nudged her knee.

"Careful!" Charlotte cried.

Elizabeth flushed with embarrassment and settled the cup and saucer more firmly on her lap.

"I apologize, Charlotte. My mind..." Her blush deepened. "...wandered. What were you saying?"

Charlotte looked at her with concern.

"I am worried about you, Eliza. You have seemed out of sorts since yesterday."

Elizabeth stared at the milk-brown beverage in her cup. It was swirling gently.

"I am well."

Charlotte "hmm-ed" non-committally.

"I also noticed you talking to yourself in the garden some days ago."

Elizabeth paused with her teacup halfway to her lips. Then she quirked her eyebrows. "I was... entertaining myself."

"I would say you are usually better at concealing the truth than that."

Elizabeth huffed.

"Well, Mr. Collins leaves me no opportunity to debate. So I took it upon myself to keep my wits sharp." She took a careful sip of her tea.

"By talking to Mr. Darcy?"

Elizabeth almost spluttered into her cup. She could feel her face flaming. Charlotte raised an eyebrow pointedly.

"I know you are hiding something." The intensity was back in Charlotte's eyes. "Can you not trust me to aid you? It would not be right if something were to happen to you while you are in my care."

Elizabeth sighed.

"Charlotte, I beg you to trust in our friendship and not ask. It will give you sleepless nights."

Charlotte looked at her in alarm. "What is that supposed to mean!?" A deep frown of suspicion etched itself on her face. "Did you have a secret understanding with Mr. Darcy? Is this grief over what happened to him?"

"Of course not!" Elizabeth said, equally alarmed. "I have never held Mr. Darcy in any esteem. You know what he did to Mr. Wickham, and how he behaved in Meryton. What he said about me!"

Then she sighed again, setting her cup down on the table between them. "Yet... the circumstances are such that it calls to my basic humanity."

Charlotte pressed her lips.

"Eliza, I would not pry usually, but you have been unwell in sudden bursts. What am I supposed to think? Please tell me no one has importuned you."

Elizabeth shook her head and gazed out of the window. If only matters were as dramatic as what Charlotte was hinting at, it would be comical and ridiculous—*for certain!*—but not what it actually was.

The sunlight was so bright, it almost hurt her eyes. Elizabeth blinked rapidly.

"I am perfectly well, Charlotte. Perhaps I will tell you someday."

Chapter 16:

REVELATIONS

Mr. Darcy did not make an appearance that night.

Neither did he show up the next morning.

Elizabeth could not help but feel a great foreboding about his absence. Yet, she carried the unfinished letter with her—the fresh sheets she had copied out in ink—wherever she went. She hoped he would appear eventually.

...and that night too, she went to bed in her morning dress.

Not her dinner clothes. Those had gotten horribly wrinkled the last time she slept in them.

"Miss Bennet?"

Elizabeth jolted awake at the sound close to her side.

She turned her head. Mr. Darcy was kneeling on the floor next to her bed. His tall frame, suddenly, at a more companionable distance from where she lay.

Her heart hammered in her chest.

"Mr. Darcy."

She glanced at the door then back at him, hoping Maria would not hear her speaking this time. A deep blush warmed her face.

Mr. Darcy had never been this close to her before. Despite the darkness, she could see the softness in his eyes as he held her gaze. She had the sudden urge to reach out and touch his face...

That immediately made Elizabeth sit up and clear her throat.

"You have returned."

"Yes," he said, standing up.

They did not speak as she lit the candle beside her bed. Then she rubbed the sleep out of her eyes and yawned.

"Lady Catherine sent some spies to find your whereabouts while you were not here."

Mr. Darcy looked alarmed. "Spies? What do you mean?"

She threw the cover aside and stood up. "Well, one cannot call them spies precisely," she said. "They were simply a pair of footmen recruited for the task. But they were meant to tail the messenger who came with news of you, and discover where you are convalescing."

The alarm on Mr. Darcy's face intensified. Elizabeth suppressed a sigh as she remembered the tea at Rosings earlier that day.

"You will be glad to know Colonel Fitzwilliam's man sent them packing. Her ladyship was very upset about it, understandably." She wondered how many more of such engagements at Rosings she would have to endure before her eventual return to Longbourn.

Bewilderment and doubt quickly crossed Mr. Darcy's face. Then a quiet thoughtfulness settled over it.

"I am not dead?"

He sounded unsure. Elizabeth bit her lip.

"I do not know, Mr. Darcy. I hope that is so... and the message did say you are beginning to heal. But..." She eyed him. "It does not explain how you are here."

Mr. Darcy dropped his gaze to the floor. Elizabeth picked up the candle and carried it to her writing desk.

"Shall we proceed with the letter? I believe we are nearly done with it."

She gazed at him over her shoulder. Mr. Darcy was still standing where she had left him.

Then, he looked at her. There was an odd intensity in his eyes. She raised her brows.

"If you would not mind, Miss Bennet, I would like to dictate a different letter to my cousin," he said.

Elizabeth could feel her brows climbing higher.

"Do you mean... we should start afresh?"

"No, just my portion."

A grimness had begun to settle over Mr. Darcy's face. It disconcerted Elizabeth as she sat down on her chair.

"Very well, Mr. Darcy. You may speak when you are ready."
She pulled some rough sheets towards herself and reached for a
pencil.

He did.

Richard,

*I do not have time to beat around the bush, so I shall only
mention what will confirm my identity to you in the quickest manner.
I refer to Ramsgate.*

*You know what Wickham attempted to do with Georgiana.
You know that the only people privy to it will never break our confidence. Not Matthew, the groom, Ellis, the footman, or Georgiana's
maid, Lucy. You know Wickham and Mrs. Younge tried to extract
five hundred pounds for their silence after asking for three thousand
at first. How you gave Wickham a good hiding and a broken nose
when you arrived shortly after.*

*I do not know if Miss Bennet will keep our confidence. I hope
she does. I believe she will. But I cannot think of anything else that
will make you consider this odd circumstance with the seriousness it
demands. Because I demand it of you.*

*If you believe me, come to Lady Catherine's parson's house in
Hunsford. I shall have a letter ready for Georgiana by the time you
do. I do not believe I will live long, if I am not dead already.*

*This miracle—for I cannot call it anything else, shall be my
last words to you. I hope you will be a good guardian to Georgie and*

keep her away from the wastrels of the peerage. Do not let her marry someone who only wants Pemberley. And, for God's sake, do not let Lady Catherine meddle! Or your mother and father for that matter. Definitely do not let Lawrence Delaney near her. I stand by what I said about him.

You are a good man, Richard. I shall miss your sorry face but let us not meet on the other side anytime soon. I shall watch from above for the day your mother successfully gets you hitched and off the battlefield. God bless.

Yours faithfully &c.
Fitzwilliam Darcy

Elizabeth stopped writing and clutched the pencil tightly in her hand.

She knew her face was wet from crying near-silent tears but she could not bring herself to move an inch. Or look up. Her heart raced in her chest.

"Miss Bennet?"

Elizabeth shook her head and swallowed the lump in her throat.

"Forgive me," Mr. Darcy said gently. "It was not my intention to distress you."

"Think nothing of it, sir," she said, at last. Then she looked at him fiercely.

"*Why* would you let him spread rumours about you in Meryton?"

Mr. Darcy searched her eyes. He raised a questioning brow.

"Mr. Wickham," she clarified.

He grimaced.

"I was not privy to what was being said about me."

Elizabeth got up from her seat and walked to the nightstand where she stored her handkerchieves. She could not bear to look at Mr. Darcy anymore. Shame swept through her as she roughly pulled out a drawer and reached for a piece of embroidered linen.

How could she have believed everything Mr. Wickham said? On such slight acquaintance that too!

"Where should I send the finished letter?"

The handkerchief—recently wet from the tears on her face—rested in a fist. Elizabeth stared at the wood grains on the top of the nightstand, keeping her back to Mr. Darcy.

"To Matlock House in Mayfair."

She nodded.

"I shall post it in the morning."

When she finally had the courage to turn around, Mr. Darcy was not in the room anymore. Elizabeth felt her heart twinge painfully.

She hoped that would not be the last time she saw him. More tears trailed down her face.

Chapter 17:

STARK

T he next few days were a blur for Elizabeth.

She would wake earlier than usual, go for a walk with paper and pencil in her reticule, sometimes find Mr. Darcy (usually near the cherry trees), and then either walk with him or write the letter for Miss Georgiana Darcy. It was the hardest thing to do.

And not just because the words would inevitably bring up strong emotions in her.

There was no knowing when Mr. Darcy would suddenly disappear. Sometimes in the middle of a sentence. Still they were plodding along and half the letter was done.

Turmoil was Elizabeth's constant companion through it all.

If anyone had asked her a few months ago to comment on Mr. Darcy's capacity to love or feel strong emotions, she would have probably scoffed and said disdain was the only acceptable emotion to such a man. She could never say such a thing anymore.

Not after writing his letter to his sister.

It was so full of love that Elizabeth found herself crying to sleep every night.

She could not imagine what Miss Darcy would feel on receiving such a missive. On knowing that her dear brother was dying. Or already dead.

And walking with Mr. Darcy made Elizabeth's own heart twist in despair, knowing that he was not long for this world. It brought on tears so frequently that she had stopped feeling embarrassed about it in his company.

She wondered what she would have made of it if she had known—six months ago—all that would transpire between them. Perhaps she would have scoffed at that too.

Oh, how she loved laughing at the follies of others!

It was what made her her father's favourite. Their shared love of catching the absurd in full display. But Elizabeth did not think she could be so flippant anymore.

...it felt like a fool's way of dallying with the world.

Chapter 18:

THE COLONEL

On the nineteenth day from the moment she saw Mr. Darcy's apparition for the first time under the cherry trees, something changed.

Elizabeth woke early as usual.

But soon she was engulfed in a furore when a certain Colonel Fitzwilliam showed up at the parsonage looking for her.

"Lady Catherine will be so pleased to see you have arrived with news!"

Mr. Collins prattled away as Charlotte settled them all in the parlour with tea and scones. Elizabeth took the chair next to Maria. It was at an angle from the Colonel and afforded her the chance to observe him without the full force of the realization that something would transpire very soon. Something unknowable.

"I hope Mr. Darcy has been recovering well," Mr. Collins continued. "We have had him in our thoughts constantly. I was inspired to lead a special prayer and sermon this past Sunday to bring her ladyship some comfort during these tough times. If I may be so bold, Lady Catherine was especially pleased with it."

He picked up a scone from the plate Charlotte was offering to everyone.

"She said to me, 'Mr. Collins, you have outdone yourself on behalf of my nephew!' And I said to her, 'It is but my duty, your ladyship, as a man of the cloth. The lifelong pursuit of offering sustenance to the spirit, and bringing the word of God as succour against the darkening of hope, is but the noblest of actions one might do.'"

He eyed the scone in his hand for a brief moment, before he—very clearly—chose to forgo *his sustenance* in order to speak some more.

"I do believe, if I say so myself, that the role of a clergyman never truly ends. One must be ever ready to tend to his flock. And more so the munificent patroness—as everyone in Hunsford and the surrounds recognizes Lady Catherine to be—during her own period of tribulation."

Mr. Collins eyed the scone again.

"I believe the sermon brought some comfort to Miss de Bourgh, however small and humble," he continued. "It must be quite the distress to know her betrothed lies indisposed in locales unknown. It would surely be a relief to her to know such little details. Would you not agree, sir?"

Mr. Collins finally took a bite of the scone while fixing a hopeful look on Colonel Fitzwilliam.

The eagerness to discover such an elusive—and invaluable—detail for Lady Catherine was undisguised on his face. His jowls moved rapidly, crunching the scone between his teeth in a manner that Elizabeth always found repugnant yet riveting. She held her peace and sipped her tea.

It had not escaped her notice how Mr. Collins had left out, from his rather long-winded speech, all the criticisms Lady Catherine had heaped on him after the aforementioned (and dubiously honourable) Sunday service.

Criticisms that included the state of dress of the congregation, their lack of volubility, and the church needing a thorough cleaning of the stained glass windows. *How else were their prayers supposed to reach the Almighty?*

"Yes, well, I thank you for your efforts," Colonel Fitzwilliam said, and then he glanced at Elizabeth.

He had been eyeing her discreetly ever since they had been introduced. Elizabeth could not fault it. She had, after all, sent him a rather outlandish letter… when they were not even acquainted with each other.

"Would you like some more tea, sir?" Charlotte asked the Colonel.

The conversation soon drifted to more pleasant subjects.

Elizabeth tried to participate. But the burning desire to find out what had happened to Mr. Darcy reduced her contributions to inanities and monosyllables.

She wondered if Colonel Fitzwilliam would ask her about her letter in present company. Or allude to it. She hoped he would not.

The possibility of facing a ruinous reputation had not been so stark to her while she was helping Mr. Darcy. But it had, suddenly, become more apparent with the cousin of the man sitting in the parsonage's parlour and enjoying Charlotte's hospitality.

It unsettled Elizabeth the longer the pleasantries and conversations went on.

...and then the Colonel proposed a walk outside.

Chapter 19:

AFFRONTED SENSIBILITIES

"I shall be but a moment!"

Mr. Collins was some paces behind them, huffing and puffing most alarmingly, as he tried to catch his breath.

"Brisk exercising—as Lady Catherine says—is essential for keeping the spirits well!"

Elizabeth glanced over her shoulder as a significant yowl of distress emerged from Mr. Collins. He was hunched over slightly as Charlotte patted him on the back.

"Is everything well?" she called out.

"I am well!" Mr. Collins wheezed, even as Maria shrugged at her helplessly from Charlotte's other side.

"Mrs. Collins, if you do not mind, I shall walk ahead with Miss Bennet," Colonel Fitzwilliam said. "I have been astride my mount for too long."

Elizabeth glanced at him surreptitiously.

Colonel Fitzwilliam—in a bid to separate her from the rest of the party—had steadily increased their walking pace from a gentle amble to a decided saunter, and then a brisk stride.

She had kept pace with him. After all, she was used to walking long distances. But it was not as if she could have fallen behind. The Colonel had offered his arm to her at the gate of the parsonage, right as they were setting off on their "short ramble along the greens", and she had been holding onto it ever since.

What Colonel Fitzwilliam had *not* anticipated was Mr. Collins' determination to remain in conversant distance with him...

Another wheeze and yowl reached them.

...that was, until the task of talking and walking had folded Mr. Collins over.

"Yes, do go on!" Charlotte said, waving them on. "We shall follow once Mr. Collins has had a moment to himself."

So they did. Even as Mr. Collins' breathless complaint "... but I am... well.." wafted in the wind behind them.

There was only silence for a while as Elizabeth and Colonel Fitzwilliam walked.

Their pace was brisk still. Small rocks and dirt crunched under their feet, and the sounds of Kentish countryside surrounded them. Elizabeth glanced at her companion.

"Shall we adopt a more leisurely pace, sir?"

Maria and the Collinses were quite behind them. Colonel Fitzwilliam glanced over his shoulder, and then fixed a shrewd look on her. "Very well, Miss Bennet."

Elizabeth sighed when they slowed down. But it did not appear as if the Colonel would broach the subject of Mr. Darcy anytime soon.

So she did.

"I believe there is something we must discuss."

Colonel Fitzwilliam nodded, keeping his eyes fixed ahead.

"I shall not beat around the bush, Miss Bennet," he said. "You claimed in your letter that you can see the spirit of my cousin Darcy?"

Skepticism was clear on his face when his eyes finally met hers. Elizabeth pursed her lips.

"I do not know if I would put it that way. But, yes, that is the essence of it," she said. "Mr. Darcy's apparition has been communicating with me for a little more than two weeks."

Her free hand strayed to where her reticule usually hung on her other arm. But there was nothing there that day. She had left it behind in the parsonage. Elizabeth dropped her hand to her side.

"We are uncertain if he... is truly departed... or if it is some anomaly heretofore unknown."

She looked at Colonel Fitzwilliam expectantly, hoping for an answer to the last. A singular "hmm" was the only response she received.

They continued to walk down the main thoroughfare, lined with poplar trees on either side.

"Is this apparition here with us right now?" Colonel Fitzwilliam asked eventually.

Elizabeth looked about her. Only the sight of sunlit trees and greens greeted her. "I am afraid not. But Mr. Darcy usually appears in the morning around this time, or sometimes in the late afternoon."

Her eyes strayed to the path in the distance that curved towards the avenue with the cherry trees. "He may yet appear."

Colonel Fitzwilliam "hmmm-ed" once more and checked his pocketwatch. "It will be nine soon."

They continued to walk in silence for some more moments. Elizabeth frowned. The day was beginning to get warm and she was beginning to get exasperated at what appeared to be total disinterest on the Colonel's part to pursue the matter further. She decided to hurry things along.

"Sir, I know all this must appear quite mad but I assure you I have only a slight acquaintance with Mr. Darcy," she said, looking at him insistently. "If you have read the letter I sent you, you must know what it contained. I was not privy to any of the matters Mr. Darcy wished me to write until he dictated them to me. He only wishes to have his words conveyed to his sister. Though, I must admit, Miss Darcy's letter is not ready yet."

Another "hmmm".

Elizabeth tried to rein in her impatience.

"Is that not why you came to the parsonage?"

Colonel Fitzwilliam's eyes glinted like steel as they settled on hers. "I came to take my measure of you."

Elizabeth was taken aback for a moment. And then she glared at him.

"And what conclusion have you arrived at?"

"That is yet to be seen," he said, sarcasm rife in his words.

"I was not born yesterday, Miss Bennet," he continued. "I believe we both know your true object behind sending me that letter. What I wish to know is how you got Darcy to tell you about Miss Georgiana Darcy. As Mr. Collins very helpfully let me know earlier, you were acquainted with my cousin earlier last year. I never believed the man's tongue could be loosened against his will. H mm?"

Elizabeth stopped walking abruptly, face burning with indignation. She removed her hand from the Colonel's arm. She knew what he had implied.

"Sir, if the circumstances were not so strange, I would be gravely offended by such aspersions on my character!"

The man snorted. "So you say, Miss Bennet."

"Yes, it is indeed what I say!" She clutched at her skirts to stop her hands from trembling. "Because it is true."

"Yet it is *you* who can see Darcy while his own family cannot," Colonel Fitzwilliam said, glaring back at her. "The woman who—in your own words—has only a slight acquaintance with the man. It all seems rather fortuitous, would you not say?"

Elizabeth took in a deep breath, and tried to calm the agitation thrumming through her. She could not leave off just yet. The matter was far too important.

"I wish I could say your suspicions are invalid, and I know how all of it appears because it was difficult for me to accept at first as well when it started," she said. "But it is indeed Mr. Darcy's apparition. And the letter I sent you were in his words. At least, the portion after mine."

Elizabeth glanced behind her to see how far Maria and the Collinses were. They seemed to be strolling more peacefully, and were still at some distance from her and Colonel Fitzwilliam.

"I know not how it came to be this way, or how such a thing is possible. It boggles the mind," she continued, turning back to her suspicious companion. "All I can say is that even if you do not believe me, I would hope that you take the letter for Miss Darcy once it is done. Please do not deprive her of it!"

Colonel Fitzwilliam grimaced.

"Very good, Miss Bennet! Brilliantly done! Pulls on the heart strings and all that," he said. "But, of course, you must know that very well!" A shadow passed over his face. "How many such apparitions have you seen in the past? Perhaps a wealthy aunt of another acquaintance? Or someone's dog that passed away and wished to say goodbye to its beloved mistress? Yes?"

Elizabeth glared at him. She was at the end of her patience with the man.

"Neither! Because this is the first instance, and I would very much prefer it to be the last."

She dropped her hands from her skirts. Face burning.

"Sir, if you believed I was a fraud, why did you come all the way to Hunsford?"

The desire to turn around and storm away burned through Elizabeth. But she held herself in place, meeting Colonel Fitzwilliam's accusatory gaze with her own.

"Why not set the letter on fire?" she continued. "Would it not have been more prudent to assist your ailing cousin than to come here and participate in *all this charade*?"

"But that is where you are wrong, Miss Bennet," Colonel Fitzwilliam replied, his tone clipped, gaze thunderous. "I would like to know who told you about Georgiana and what you are planning to do with the information."

His eyes became even steelier than before.

"Or perhaps I should have you committed to Bedlam for trying to take advantage of people when they are vulnerable. It would kill two birds with a stone!"

"That's enough, Richard!"

Elizabeth gasped.

Mr. Darcy stepped around her, coming to a halt beside them. She stared at him.

There was a ringing in her ears. Seeming silence surrounded her. Blood thumped through her veins. Her heart raced.

"Am I to believe that Darcy is with us at the moment?"

Elizabeth blinked. Sensations rushed back to her.

She glanced at Colonel Fitzwilliam who was staring at her with faint mockery in his eyes. Then she looked back at Mr. Darcy. He was glaring at his cousin.

"Yes," she said, voice hoarse all of a sudden.

She turned back when Colonel Fitzwilliam started laughing. "How fortunate!"

Her face flamed.

"Richard..."

Elizabeth looked at Mr. Darcy. Grim anger was etched on his features. But also a nascent helplessness. Their eyes met.

She straightened herself to her full height—not that there was much of it to begin with. She could not be bothered with Colonel Fitzwilliam any longer.

"You said you could not see anyone else but me," she asked Mr. Darcy. A strange frisson was growing within her.

Mr. Darcy nodded. A flash of guilt crossed his face before it settled back to grimness. "I started seeing others again... the day you and Mrs. Collins were having tea in the parsonage sitting room."

Elizabeth frowned.

"Six days ago."

It only took her a moment to remember. It was all in his eyes. Elizabeth's heart squeezed painfully.

It was the day she had told Charlotte that she did not hold him in any esteem.

Because of Mr. Wickham.

Was that why he had asked her to change the letter to his cousin? Shared what he had about his sister and the blackguard?

Elizabeth's eyes blurred with unshed tears.

Colonel Fitzwilliam startled next to her. But she ignored him.

"Are you dying, Mr. Darcy?" she croaked past the lump in her throat.

"I am sorry, Miss Bennet," he said, the grimness dissolving into sadness, and even more helplessness. "...I believe so."

Was that why he kept disappearing when they tried to compose the letter for Miss Darcy?

The tears spilled over. Twin tracks on Elizabeth's cheeks.

"Miss Bennet?"

Elizabeth looked at Colonel Fitzwilliam. Then at Maria and the Collinses gaining on them. She quickly swiped at her tears.

"Is Mr. Darcy dying, sir?" she asked.

Colonel Fitzwilliam's silence, and the guarded cast to his jaws, told her everything she needed to know. She tried to compose herself.

"I am sorry, sir, I am in no condition to continue our walk," she said. "I shall have the Miss Darcy's letter ready as soon as I can. If... if you would care to collect it."

Chapter 20:

I Love You

Elizabeth did not know if Mr. Darcy followed her or chose to remain with his cousin. All she knew was that she was in no state to write any letters right then.

She simply ran to her room in the parsonage and locked the door behind her. Then she collapsed on the bed with unending tears.

In all her twenty years, Elizabeth had never been exposed to anything so raw and heartwrenching.

The deaths she had known of until then were of shallow acquaintances, or people she had not known very well. Her own grandparents on the Bennet side of the family had shuffled off the mortal coil when she was three—right after Kitty's birth. And those on Mrs. Bennet's side had been long from the world before her mother had married her father.

Even the tragedy of Napoleon's ongoing war had not truly affected the gentry of Meryton as much as it could have, though there were plenty of young men in the village and tenant houses who never returned home. The gentility were, after all, above the touch of such deaths.

Elizabeth suddenly felt exceptionally stupid as she realized—for all her satire and wise speak—she had never truly been wise at all.

Everything had brushed past her like the breeze. Unnoticed. Even when she thought she had noticed.

"Miss Bennet, I implore you, do not cry."

Elizabeth raised her head from the cocoon of her arms. Mr. Darcy was kneeling once more beside her bed, their faces close enough to touch.

"How can I not?"

Tears continued to roll down her cheeks.

Mr. Darcy searched her eyes.

"I thought you did not hold me in any esteem."

Heat flooded Elizabeth's face. She swiped roughly at her tears. The lump in her throat had grown to the size of a giant boulder.

"I did not..." she said, hoarsely. "It is true."

More tears overflowed from her eyes.

"But I do now."

Her heart was weighed down, as if full of lead. As if it would sink through the earth and all the waters, and never stop sinking. *"How could I not after spending so much time with you?"*

Raw anguish suddenly spread through Mr. Darcy's features. He disappeared. One moment there. The next moment, not.

Elizabeth covered her head with her arms once more and continued to cry.

Chapter 21:

CHARLOTTE'S CONFESSION

That night, after dinner, Charlotte drew Elizabeth aside. She had that look in her eyes. The one that said she had just discovered something big.

"Is it true, Eliza?"

Elizabeth raised her eyebrows in question.

"Can you see..." Charlotte paused and looked behind them. The corridor was in no danger of suddenly hosting any more people other than them. She turned back to Elizabeth, but lowered her voice some more.

"Mr. Darcy's spirit? Do you see him?"

Elizabeth froze. She could feel the blood draining from her face. But she tried to strike nonchalance as best as she could.

"What do you mean, Charlotte?"

It was Charlotte's turn to raise her brows. And she did so quite decisively.

"Colonel Fitzwilliam told me."

Of course!

Elizabeth grit her teeth as blood rushed back to her face.

"If I could, that would be a tale for the ages, would it not?" she said lightly, even as her hands clenched her skirts to compose herself. She huffed. "I cannot fathom why the Colonel would say such a thing!"

"Yes, it did sound odd to me at first," Charlotte said. But there was that *other look* in her eyes that Elizabeth knew all too well. The two stared at each other for a long moment. Neither willing to back down.

And then—all of a sudden—Charlotte reached between them and took Elizabeth's hands in hers. "I believe you."

Elizabeth's eyes widened in surprise.

But she quickly hid it behind her usual pleasantness.

"I truly do not know what you mean. Surely you do not believe such a thing!" She drew her hands out of Charlotte's grasp, even as the latter fixed her with a look of exasperation.

"Eliza, I believe we have been friends long enough that I know when you are lying."

"Well, I am not this time!" Elizabeth said. "Perhaps we should talk in the morning. It has been a tiring day."

She started to walk away. And she was nearly at the foot of the staircase—when Charlotte spoke again.

"Would you tell me, then, why you sent a letter to Matlock House last week?"

Elizabeth stilled. And then she bit her lip, hard.

Of course nothing ever stayed a secret in country villages!

She turned around. Charlotte had that stubborn cast to her face. Elizabeth knew it mirrored her own.

"Why?" she asked.

Her heart was thumping loudly in her chest. The now-familiar ache, spreading through her bones. She did not wish to speak of this.

"Why would you believe such a thing?"

There was a pressure building behind her eyes.

Charlotte's face softened. She closed the distance between them.

"Because I know you, Eliza, and you are not one for such fanciful notions."

"Neither are you."

A small smile appeared on Charlotte's face.

"Yes, but I have caught you speaking to thin air a couple of times when you did not know," she said. "And, to tell the truth, I was rather relieved when Colonel Fitzwilliam mentioned what he did to me."

Her smile dimmed.

"I believed it was something entirely different. I was beginning to worry."

Elizabeth stared at her. "He threatened to have me sent to Bedlam."

A stricken look appeared on Charlotte's face.

"Who?"

"Colonel Fitzwilliam."

"Oh Eliza!"

Charlotte instantly drew Elizabeth into a hug.

Elizabeth stiffened. But then she leaned into Charlotte, placing her arms around her friend. The strain she had not realized she was feeling inside unravelled.

"I still do not understand why you believe such a thing," Elizabeth whispered. "Nobody would."

Twin tears rolled down her cheeks.

Charlotte tightened her hold around Elizabeth.

"I never told anyone this," Charlotte said, her voice almost in Elizabeth's hair. "But when I was twelve and Grandmother Lucas had just passed away, I saw her ghost twice at the top of the landing. Outside the room that used to be hers."

"What?"

Elizabeth pulled back, clutching at Charlotte's arms in disbelief. "Truly?"

Charlotte nodded. A wry smile appeared on her face. Then she laughed mirthlessly.

"The way I strayed far from that room. For months! And then Aunt Petunia visited us, and mother gave her that room, and nothing much happened. So I began to wonder if I had imagined the whole thing."

A bubble of relieved laughter escaped Elizabeth.

"Oh Charlotte!"

She continued to laugh. And then wiped the tears from her face. "I cannot believe you saw Grandmother Lucas' ghost."

"I did," Charlotte shrugged, grinning. But there was kindness on her face alongside that knowing look.

"Would you care to have some tea?"

The two of them simply held each other's gaze for a moment. Then Elizabeth nodded.

"I would like that very much."

Chapter 22:

STONE MAN

"You must forgive me, Miss Bennet, if I was especially harsh in my words yesterday."

Elizabeth was silent for a moment, contemplative eyes fixed ahead as she walked.

Morning light bathed the shrubs and grass on either side of the road, and the tops of the more distant trees; some of which were flowering. Some were not. The gentle scent of spring was in the air.

"What changed your mind?"

"I cannot say that my mind is changed," Colonel Fitzwilliam said. "But I wished to give you a fair chance to speak your piece."

They walked in silence for some more time.

Earlier that day, when Elizabeth had left the parsonage for her usual morning constitutional (reticule in hand, in case Mr. Darcy appeared later), she had chanced upon the Colonel not too far from the head of the road. She did not believe it was a coincidence.

"There is not much to say, I am afraid," Elizabeth said, breaking her silence. "I shall give you the letter for Miss Darcy once it is ready. You may do with it as you believe is right."

Colonel Fitzwilliam glanced at her. But she kept her eyes fixed ahead.

"Did Darcy say anything to you yesterday?" he asked, and then cleared his throat. "You seemed distressed when you left. It was quite abrupt."

And why might that be?

Elizabeth did not vocalize her thoughts. "He did not."

They walked in silence for some moments more.

"How is Mr. Darcy faring?" she asked after a while. "This matter has been kept quite secretive thus far, if I am being perfectly honest."

"Yes, it has," Colonel Fitzwilliam said. "We have our reasons."

"Would it have anything to do with Lady Catherine?"

Another glance was cast her way.

"Yes, and no."

Elizabeth almost threw up her hands in annoyance, but a deep frown did etch itself on her lips. She fixed a glare on the Colonel. "Sir, you may not believe I can see your cousin's apparition, but the poor man deserves to know what happened to him!"

Colonel Fitzwilliam simply "hmm-ed".

Then he said, "Perhaps I shall tell him once I have satisfied my curiosity. You could act as our intermediary, could you not? I would like to ask him a few questions first."

Elizabeth sighed.

"Yes, I can do that. But I do not know when Mr. Darcy will appear."

"Well then, one can only hope Darcy will make an appearance sooner rather than later."

Elizabeth rolled her eyes and looked away.

Colonel Fitzwilliam very much still believed she was a fraud.

Chapter 23:

IDYLL

Later that day when Elizabeth had a moment to herself, she leaned against the window in her room and chewed on her lips.

Mr. Darcy had made an appearance near the end of her walk. But the task of being an intermediary had not gone as smoothly as she had hoped.

...not between Colonel Fitzwilliam's open suspicion of everything she conveyed and Mr. Darcy's rapid frustrations at his "pig-headed cousin".

But she had bigger problems.

Lady Catherine had sent new summons as usual.

She wished everyone at the parsonage to join her at Rosings later that evening and stay for dinner. Elizabeth was certain she would create a spectacle of the grandest proportions—with the help of Mr. Collins' endless sycophantism—to convince Colonel Fitzwilliam to take her and Miss de Bourgh wherever Mr. Darcy was hidden away. Elizabeth did not wish to suffer through hours of that.

Not that she had a choice.

Her mind wandered to the unfinished letter for Miss Darcy. She was beginning to have an awful suspicion in the depths of her stomach. Especially with Mr. Darcy's appearances so unpredictable these days. And so much shorter.

Colonel Fitzwilliam's tight-lipped stance did not bode well either. Elizabeth was afraid that she would see Mr. Darcy for the last time any day now.

She squeezed her eyes shut.

The perfect idyll outside her window was no longer comforting.

Chapter 24:

CRESCENDO

"**B**ut that is unacceptable!"

Lady Catherine stabbed the carpeted floor repeatedly with her walking staff. Her voice was rather shrill that day, though it had not lost any of her domineering strength.

"I have never been subjected to such mistreatment! And you know right well, nephew, I will not begin now!"

"There is always a first time," Colonel Fitzwilliam said.

He was the picture of nonchalance.

In fact, he looked so unbothered that Elizabeth wondered if he was truly bored or simply putting on an act. She eyed him from her seat on the opposite side of the parlour.

Perhaps it was to be expected. Lady Catherine was more than what most could bear.

"On my life, I have never!"

Anger and disbelief vied for control on the older lady's face. The former won out.

"What I believe her ladyship is attempting to convey is how delicate the matter has become," Mr. Collins said quickly. "Colonel Fitzwilliam, I entreat you to act without hesitation! God is witness to the misfortunes cast upon Miss de Bourgh. What must be going through the heart of a mother to watch her child be so bereaved!"

Elizabeth glanced at Miss de Bourgh. The latter appeared just as unbothered as her cousin, resting as she was on her usual settee near the fireplace. Her eyes were fixed on the crackling flames. A blankness in them.

"That is quite enough, Mr. Collins!"

Lady Catherine thumped her staff on the carpet again.

"As you say, your ladyship!"

Mr. Collins shrank back in his seat.

"I simply cannot understand the cause for such stubbornness, nephew!" Lady Catherine continued. "I have letters from Lord Matlock in my possession that are in agreement to this match. And Darcy himself was on his way here—as he does each year—to meet his dear Anne. You know that very well."

Her face was well and truly red.

"How can you hold us back from going to him now? When time is of the essence!"

She whacked the floor with her staff a few more times. *Thump. Thump. Thump!*

Elizabeth looked away from the diminutive creature on the settee as her heart squeezed painfully. Her fingers tightened around the handle of her tea cup.

Bitter blackness greeted her from the depths of the fine china.

"Indeed! Her ladyship is right, Colonel Fitzwilliam, as she always is!" Mr. Collins piped in. "Delay may prove most unfortunate!"

Elizabeth swallowed the lukewarm tea.

"Charlotte, I cannot bear it anymore!"

Elizabeth spoke in a whispered rush, gripping her friend's arm just as they were about to enter the parsonage.

They were returning much later than usual from Rosings. But that was to be expected.

"What is the matter, Eliza?" Charlotte looked at her with concern.

Mr. Collins and Maria had already stepped inside, and they could hear the former's voice echoing out of the open door as he berated Janet, the all-works maid, about something or another. Elizabeth pulled Charlotte closer to the flowers growing by the porch.

"Oh, Charlotte! I wish I could see him!" she said. Despair tinged her voice. She was trying hard to hold back the tears prickling in her eyes. But she knew not how much longer she would succeed.

"Mr. Darcy?" The concern on Charlotte's face grew deeper. "Why? Is something the matter?" She glanced at the open doorway. Nobody had come out yet asking after them.

"Yes," Elizabeth said, trying to compose herself. She twisted her fingers into her skirt.

"All that talk in Rosings was... well, it was distressing! And I just..." Her voice grew hoarse. "I just wish I could see Mr. Darcy in flesh, wherever he is convalescing. But I cannot. And I dread the moment his spirit disappears forever."

Elizabeth raised her eyes skywards to stop the tears she knew were imminent. But words kept pouring out of her.

"I just... I do not know how, Charlotte... but I feel Mr. Darcy's tether to this world is thinning."

A singular tear rolled down one cheek.

"Oh!" Elizabeth laughed without mirth, swiping at it. "I cannot believe I have become such a watering pot! What a wretch I am!"

"Oh, Eliza..." Charlotte whispered, gripping her hand tightly.

Elizabeth looked at her friend. "I just–"

"*Charlotte!*" Mr. Collins' voice rang out, moments before he stepped out of the house, onto the porch.

He frowned at both of them.

"Is something the matter? Come inside, the two of you! I do not want cold air to get in!"

"Yes dear, we shall be there in a moment," Charlotte said quickly. "Do go in."

Mr. Collins "hmm-ed", eyeing Elizabeth suspiciously, before he went back inside. Charlotte turned back to her.

"I shall come to your room later. Wait for me, please." She squeezed Elizabeth's hand once more.

"...there might be something I can do."

Chapter 25:

Unspoken

When Elizabeth stepped into her room upstairs, she realized she was not alone.

"Mr. Darcy!" she said, startled.

She quickly glanced behind her in the corridor. No one had heard her. But Maria and Janet were discussing something at the head of the stairs.

She quickly closed the door. Then she turned back to face him. The two of them stared at each other.

Elizabeth could feel her face beginning to warm.

Had he heard her earlier? When she was speaking to Charlotte?

She cleared her throat.

"When did you arrive?"

She stepped deeper into the room and set her reticule on a side table.

"Just some..." Mr. Darcy paused. "Uh... now."

Elizabeth raised her brows. *Was Mr. Darcy lying?* Her face warmed some more.

"I was at Rosings," she said.

"Yes."

He blushed immediately. And then added, "I heard Mr. Collins..."

Elizabeth could feel herself blushing even more furiously now. *He was lying!* She was certain.

"Well, then." She did not know what to say.

Her gaze flitted around the room, never staying on anything in particular. Not the curtains. Not the floorboards. Not the writing desk. Most definitely not on Mr. Darcy!

"How was your dinner?" he asked.

Their eyes met.

Elizabeth could feel her face burning. Flaming. *An inferno!* She had the sudden desire to run outside and walk, and walk, and walk in the night chill until she was an icicle instead.

"It was... pleasant."

They stared at each other.

"I was–"

"Did you–"

They spoke at the same time.

Both blushed furiously once more.

"You first, Miss Bennet," he said.

"Oh... no, it is not of..." Elizabeth started, before trailing off. She gazed at Mr. Darcy.

At his dark eyes. The proud, aristocratic nose. The familiar curl of hair on one side of his forehead. The shape of his chin. Her heart squeezed.

She stood frozen. Unable to look away.

She had never felt this way before.

...and soon it would not matter.

"It is of no import..." Elizabeth said at last. Her voice was just a touch above a whisper—strained with the effort to not let her sorrow seep in.

She would never see him again.

Elizabeth knew she had not succeeded when Mr. Darcy's eyes widened. He took a step towards her. And then he stopped. He looked unsure of what to do with his hands.

Bitterness washed across his features. He dropped his gaze, fixing it on the floor between them.

It had never felt more like a chasm to Elizabeth.

"I should... let you refresh yourself," he said.

"No," she said, at once.

Mr. Darcy looked up in surprise.

Elizabeth shrugged. A weak smile appeared on her face, even as she clutched at her skirts. She walked to the writing desk, stepping around him.

"I think we should finish your letter to Miss Darcy."

Chapter 26:

CHARLOTTE'S WAY

F ate does not always unfold infinitesimally.

Sometimes, it unfolds all at once.

When Charlotte knocked on Elizabeth's door later that same night, the latter was in the middle of writing Miss Darcy's letter, with Mr. Darcy seated near her in his usual chair.

"Eliza, I have news!" Charlotte said as she hurried in and closed the door behind her. She was still dressed in the gown she had worn to Rosings.

"News?" Elizabeth asked, glancing discreetly at Mr. Darcy.

"Yes," Charlotte said, and then paused. Her eyes swept over Elizabeth's clothes. "You are not in your nightclothes. That is good! I was worried you might be."

"Yes, well…" Elizabeth cleared her throat. "Why?"

"I shall tell you in a minute. Let me catch my breath."

Charlotte walked deeper into the room and started for the chair where Mr. Darcy was sitting. A look of alarm flashed across both Elizabeth and his face.

"Not that!"

Elizabeth quickly stepped in front of Charlotte and physically maneuvered her friend into the chair she had occupied just moments ago.

"Sit here! It is more comfortable."

"Eliza!"

Charlotte huffed in exasperation.

And then her eyes fell on the papers on the desk.

A frown etched itself between Charlotte's brows. Her gaze shifted to the other chair. The one with Mr. Darcy... who looked even more uncomfortable than he had before. He quickly vacated the seat.

"Eliza?" Charlotte asked, slowly turning her gaze on Elizabeth. "Is Mr. Darcy here?"

Elizabeth felt her face flame.

"Well..."

"He is, is he not?!" Charlotte cried, glancing at Mr. Darcy's chair again. She threw up her hands and stood up.

"On my word, Eliza! I do not like this."

"Charlotte, please," Elizabeth said quickly. "It is not–"

"Eliza, unmarried men and women cannot be alone without a chaperone," Charlotte said, exasperation clear on her face. "I always believed you were meeting outside." She glared at the empty chair. "Surely you are aware of that, sir."

Mr. Darcy—who was standing next to it—flushed bright red.

Charlotte threw her hands up again, perhaps at the ridiculousness of speaking to thin air, and turned back to Elizabeth. "Can he hear me?"

"Charlotte..." Elizabeth began.

"Mrs. Collins is not wrong, Miss Bennet."

Elizabeth looked at Mr. Darcy.

He shifted uncomfortably. Guilt and embarrassment were clearly marked on his face.

"It was not my intention to make you feel importuned."

"Eliza?"

Elizabeth turned back to Charlotte. The latter had her eyebrows arched.

"Can Mr. Darcy hear me?" she asked again.

"I will be outside," Mr. Darcy said.

Elizabeth huffed in annoyance—looking from one to another. She held up a hand.

"Can the two of you give me a moment to speak?!"

A beat of awkward silence spread through the room.

Mr. Darcy looked conflicted. Charlotte affronted.

Elizabeth sighed.

"Charlotte, nothing untoward has happened between me and Mr. Darcy," she said. "Surely you can see these are extraordinary circumstances?"

Then she added quickly—on seeing the still-affronted look on Charlotte's face and the deepening guilt on his: "Mr. Darcy has never broken propriety with me... other than what could not be avoided."

She looked in his direction. He was staring at the floor-boards, hands in his coat pockets.

"...I was helping him write a letter."

Silence permeated the room once more. The only sound, that of a distant owl hooting somewhere outside the window.

Charlotte "hmm-ed" after a beat. Elizabeth frowned at her in exasperation. "You had some news, Charlotte, did you not?"

Mr. Darcy raised his head.

"Yes," Charlotte answered, a half-uncertain, half-disapproving cast to her brows as she glanced at the empty chair again.

"I have found a way for you to visit Mr. Darcy."

And so, there they were.

"How did you do it?"

Elizabeth asked Charlotte as the covered cart they were in rattled and bumped along the road.

Their pace was slow enough to not risk danger in the darkness—and relative quiet—of the night. Yet fast enough so they could reach their destination in a few hours. Elizabeth did not know where they were going though.

"It is something only Mrs. Collins can do," Charlotte replied, in her usual ironic self-confidence.

Elizabeth rolled her eyes.

It was just like her friend to persuade the most un-persuadable to do as she wished. She peered through the tiny window on her side at Colonel Fitzwilliam on horseback.

He, and two other footmen from Rosings, were accompanying them on the journey that had unfolded in the most dramatic—albeit clandestine—manner.

As it turned out, Lady Catherine had some people on her employ who were more loyal to her nephews than the lady-ship herself. But the cart belonged to a parishioner who owed Charlotte a large kindness. After all, they could not risk taking a carriage from Rosings.

Elizabeth did not know how Charlotte had managed to arrange it all. But she had.

And so there she was.

Sitting beside Charlotte—cloth bag with some bare necessities and a change of clothes near her feet—bumping along on the main highway, with Mr. Collins and Maria sleeping soundly far behind in the parsonage and none the wiser.

"I must say, I never imagined I would do something like this."

Elizabeth turned back to Charlotte. Her voice was a hushed whisper in the stark silence. "Least of all with you!"

"Why not? Is *Mrs. Collins* too practical to do such a thing?"

"Stop that, Charlotte! You know what I mean."

They were silent for some more moments. Each lost in their own thoughts.

"What I cannot believe is finding Mr. Darcy in your room," Charlotte said.

Elizabeth's cheeks grew heated.

"You say that as if you found us in the middle of something compromising," she retorted.

"Perhaps not."

Charlotte turned to give Elizabeth her full attention. There was an unsettling pity in her eyes.

"But, Eliza, I must caution you to not catch feelings for the man. However extraordinary the circumstances might be, it may not turn out as you wish."

Elizabeth bit her lip.

"Besides, it would not be prudent even if Mr. Darcy was not on his deathbed," Charlotte added.

Silence descended between them once more.

Elizabeth stared out of the window at the distant outline of dark trees. The cart continued to rattle along the road. Its wheels seemed to dip into every pothole! Her heart ached.

"Why not?" she asked after a while.

Her voice was uncharacteristically small.

"Hmm?" Charlotte looked at her. And then her expression settled into one of gentle kindness.

Elizabeth did not like it one bit... even in the shadowy gloom of the lantern lights swinging outside the cart.

"Because, unlike Mrs. Collins and her practicality," Charlotte said, taking her hand. "You, my dear Eliza, deserve more than an attachment born from extraordinary circumstances."

Tears prickled in Elizabeth's eyes.

"You would not be happy without true love."

Chapter 27:

LIMINAL SPACES

In some time less than three hours, their cart reached a small hamlet that was several villages inland from the main highway to London.

Elizabeth gaped as they passed a minuscule square with a single inn and one general store, plunked right next to a rather miserable looking smithy.

"The accident occurred near Dunhill bridge, did it not?"

"Yes," Charlotte said.

They had passed it sometime ago.

Elizabeth wondered how many more villages they might pass before Colonel Fitzwilliam brought their cart to a halt.

And why so far inland?

Would it not have been more advisable to keep the injured closer to the highway?

But what did she know of what Mr. Darcy's family had on their mind. Elizabeth rested her head against the window.

Perhaps she was overestimating the distance.

Perhaps it only seemed so because their cart was crawling forward at a pace that Lydia and Kitty might outstrip on foot.

Perhaps she could–

"Ho boy!"

Elizabeth startled out of her thoughts as the cart suddenly came to a grinding halt, nearly flinging her to the opposite side.

She steadied herself and looked out of the window.

A quaint two-storey cottage home, surrounded by maple trees, stood to one side of the road with what looked like a small farm beyond it. But it was too dark to see anything clearly.

"This must be where they are caring for Mr. Darcy," Charlotte said, eyeing the house and the yard.

The cart door swung open just then. Colonel Fitzwilliam was framed beyond it.

He looked grim.

"We are here, ladies."

If Elizabeth had thought that she would see Mr. Darcy right after disembarking from the rickety old cart, she had thought wrong.

They would have to wait until morning.

Or so the Colonel had told them.

She sighed and tried to pay mind to whatever the matron of the house—a Mrs. Ronald—was telling her and Charlotte as she led them upstairs to a guest room. The woman appeared to be of the same age as Mrs. Bennet, with greying hair at her temples and a heavyset bearing.

"This is the room I was telling ya about," the lady said, ushering them in.

It had a basic bed that they would have to share, and a few other bare furniture. There was also a small window to one side. It would do.

"Ye will be comfortable here. But if ye need anything, call out for Bessie. She will hear ya."

Then it was just her and Charlotte.

...and then just her, lying awake in bed while Charlotte slept soundly beside her.

Despite the warm and comfortable house and their more than solicitous hostess, all Elizabeth could think of was how Mr. Darcy was right then resting somewhere close. Only some doors away.

Mrs. Ronald had informed them (on Charlotte's urging) how Mr. Darcy's valet and her younger son were charged with keeping an eye on the gentleman. They took turns at it so the other might sleep.

Apparently, Mr. Darcy jolted awake every so often, every day, for a few moments. Only to promptly lose consciousness once more. The physician was concerned about it because he did not know what was causing it. But someone needed to be there to fetch him if anything changed.

Nevertheless, since the pattern had persisted for a few weeks by then, none of them were hopeful it would get better. It worried Elizabeth.

It was too eerily close to her own experience with Mr. Darcy's apparition. But in a different way.

After a long time of simply staring at the ceiling and thinking, Elizabeth got out of the bed.

Then, she wrapped a shawl around herself and left the room.

Chapter 28:

ELIZABETH

She was staring outside the window—the one in the tiny, corner sitting room on the second floor. Staring into the inky darkness as it slowly receded to dawn.

Then, suddenly, she knew she was not alone any longer.

"Elizabeth..."

She turned.

Mr. Darcy was standing behind her.

Their eyes met, and held. And for a long while neither spoke or looked away.

"I do not... wish you to see me," he said quietly.

Elizabeth glanced at her hands.

Her fingers had begun to twist around each other. She frowned.

"I see."

"It is not a pleasant sight," Mr. Darcy said.

She stared at the folds of his cravat.

His valet must have spent considerable time crafting it to refined elegance.

"Elizabeth–"

"I brought the letter to Miss Darcy with me. The rough pages," she said.

She did not wish to think or feel what she was trying hard not to think or feel. The intensity thrumming between them was making it hard to do.

Elizabeth looked away and walked to the small table where she had left her reticule. She could not part from it these days. Then, she sat down on an armchair, drawing the partially-filled papers out from within the folds of the bag.

When Mr. Darcy did not say anything for a long while, Elizabeth looked up. He was staring at her with sadness in his eyes.

"Mr. Darcy?"

She attempted to strike a nonchalant tone, but failed. She looked away again.

"Why did you come?" he asked.

There was a strained edge to his voice.

Elizabeth swallowed the lump in her throat, and shrugged.

"Seemed like the thing to do."

She could feel her eyes prickling again. She did not think she would be able to stay composed for too long.

She stared at the pencil-marked pages. The words twisted and danced before her eyes, failing to mean anything to her. They were simply a bunch of curling inscriptions in dull grey.

...and then a thought struck her.

"You were able to leave Hunsford!"

Mr. Darcy was staring at the floorboards.

"Yes."

She bit her lip, and stared at her hands as they rested on the pages on her lap. This confirmed what she had begun to believe about their strange circumstance but had not dared to hope.

"Did you... visit yourself?" she asked.

"Yes."

Elizabeth looked up in alarm at the strangled quality in his voice. *How bad was it?*

Her heart tugged painfully. There was a grimness on Mr. Darcy's face.

"Miss Bennet?"

Elizabeth startled.

Colonel Fitzwilliam was standing at the partially ajar door of the room, dressed in his nightclothes with a robe thrown on top. He was eyeing the room strangely. Warily. His shrewd eyes landed on hers.

"I could not sleep," she said quickly, even as heat rushed to her cheeks.

"Is he here? Darcy?"

There was a hesitation in the Colonel's voice. Like he did not wish to believe... but somehow did. *What had Charlotte said to him?!*

Elizabeth glanced at Mr. Darcy.

Their eyes held for a moment. She nodded.

"Ah, I see."

Silence descended in the room as Colonel Fitzwilliam gingerly stepped in. As if he was afraid to set something off.

Elizabeth clutched the pages in her hands as she glanced between the cousins. One in flesh. The other in spirit. They both did not seem to know where to look.

"Would you like to visit Darcy right now?" Colonel Fitzwilliam asked. "Seeing as we are both awake."

His eyes swept the room once more.

"I meant Darcy's sick bed."

"Yes," Elizabeth said.

"No," Mr. Darcy said.

She glared at him.

"Miss Bennet, please do not..." Mr. Darcy said. His eyes beseeched her.

She looked away.

"It is Miss Bennet now, is it?"

She set down the pages on the armchair and stood up. When she looked at him again, Mr. Darcy looked embarrassed.

"Elizabeth..."

She focused on Colonel Fitzwilliam instead. The man was scrutinizing the spot where Mr. Darcy stood.

"Lead the way, sir, if you please."

Chapter 29:

HANDS

It did not take them long to make their way to the room where Mr. Darcy was being housed.

It was on the first floor of the cottage. Easier to reach. But not in the way.

A young man opened the door when the Colonel knocked. He looked like he was in his early twenties, and had a distinct similarity in appearance to Mrs. Ronald. He gawked at them in surprise.

"Dennis, you can return at the strike of the hour. I shall be here until then," Colonel Fitzwilliam said.

Then he turned to Elizabeth.

"Miss Bennet, it is not a pretty sight. I will not hold it against you if you do not wish to see."

"I wish to see," Elizabeth said simply.

Colonel Fitzwilliam sighed.

They went in.

A powerful feeling seized Elizabeth as soon as she laid eyes on the man on the narrow bed.

It was Mr. Darcy.

A heavily bandaged version of him, with a purple bruise-covered face that was swollen around the eyes and nose.

She gasped and placed a hand over her mouth. Tears blurred her vision. It was indeed awful!

"He stirs every now and then," Colonel Fitzwilliam said, leading her deeper into the room. "But Dr. Goodman is not sure why he has not woken yet."

Elizabeth glanced at Mr. Darcy's apparition as he stepped into the room behind them. Her heart thumped heavily in her chest. The man looked pale as he stared at his own broken form on the bed.

She turned back to the prone man in flesh. Mr. Darcy did not look as if he was at peace, even though he appeared to be sleeping. She felt her tears brim over and roll down her cheeks.

She could see Colonel Fitzwilliam fidgeting next to her. Then, he stepped back.

"I shall give you a moment."

Elizabeth did not answer as the Colonel stepped out of the room, leaving the door open behind him. She could only stare at the battered gentleman on the bed.

"Please, Miss Bennet..." Mr. Darcy said softly from somewhere beside her. "I do not wish you to distress yourself."

More tears fell from her eyes. But she did not turn away.

"Elizabeth..."

She reached out and brushed a finger against his hand. The one resting on the bed, slightly out of the confines of the quilt covering him.

A sudden strangled sound made her look at Mr. Darcy, the apparition. He was staring at his hand. The same one she was touching on his body.

"You can feel it?" she asked, hesitantly.

"Yes," he breathed.

And then he looked at her with a wild intensity in his eyes. Elizabeth felt her cheeks flame. Her heart thudded violently in her chest.

She turned her attention to Mr. Darcy's prone form once more and gently held more of his hand. It rested in her grasp. Unresponsive and somewhat heavy. But warm to the touch.

It was so much larger than hers...

More tears streaked down her face.

"Miss Bennet..."

They looked at each other.

Mr. Darcy raised his hand in wonder.

"I can feel you."

And then...

—suddenly—

...he released a choking sound and grabbed at his midriff.

Elizabeth gasped in alarm.

"Mr. Darcy!"

He vanished in thin air.

Elizabeth whipped back when she felt a slight tug on her fingers. Mr. Darcy—the one on the bed—was beginning to stir. His fingers curled around hers weakly. His face twitched in pain.

"Colonel Fitzwilliam!" Elizabeth shouted. Tears continued to streak down her face.

The Colonel rushed into the room. "My God! What has happened?"

Then he stilled once his gaze fell upon Mr. Darcy... and how her fingers were wrapped around his. Something akin to pity flickered in his eyes. He sighed.

"Darcy... he, uh... he does that once or twice a day. It is nothing, Miss Bennet."

"Oh," Elizabeth said.

She knew she sounded just as crestfallen as she felt. She turned back to Mr. Darcy.

He was not moving as much as she had believed initially. Just enough to seem as if he would come awake any moment. She let go of his hand... though his fingers clutched at hers right before she pulled them away.

"I think I shall go to bed now."

She avoided meeting the Colonel's eyes as more tears rolled down her cheeks. Colonel Fitzwilliam nodded.

"Get some sleep, Miss Bennet. I shall see you in the morning."

Chapter 30:

AWAKE

When Elizabeth woke up, the whole house was in an uproar.

She leapt out of the bed and ran out of the room, rubbing sleep from her eyes.

"What is going on?" she asked, catching Mrs. Ronald at the head of the stairs. It was chaos everywhere.

"Oh dear, it is Mr. Darcy! The invalid," Mrs. Ronald said, stopping for a second. "He has woken up!"

Elizabeth gasped.

The shock dispelled every last vestige of sleep.

...but she only learnt more once she found Charlotte in the breakfast room, where the latter was sitting alone and eating plain toast with a cup of tea.

"Charlotte! Why did you not wake me?"

Elizabeth stormed into the room. Upset. *How could she have slept through the pandemonium?*

Charlotte sighed and put down the toast in her hand.

"You look so tired, Eliza. I did not have the heart to wake you. Besides, Colonel Fitzwilliam told me about your early morning visit to see Mr. Darcy."

She told Elizabeth all that she had missed.

Mr. Darcy had seemingly woken up sometime in the morning... soon after Elizabeth had gone to bed. And then a huge commotion had ensued to bring Dr. Goodman immediately from the village inn because Mr. Darcy was in tremendous pain. The groans alone had roused the entire house.

...everyone but her.

Charlotte believed that Elizabeth had been too exhausted from their bumpy travel. For, she had slept like the dead through it all. It troubled Elizabeth.

But she was glad she had missed everything once Charlotte explained how excruciating Mr. Darcy's cries were. And just how loud. It had only stopped once Dr. Goodman dosed him with some laudanum.

"At first, they debated whether or not to give him any," Charlotte said, taking another bite of her toast.

"What? *Why* would they not?" Elizabeth asked, horrified.

Charlotte looked a little green as she quickly sipped some tea. As if she was remembering the moment.

"Dr. Goodman was worried Mr. Darcy would not wake up again if he dosed him. But he capitulated at Colonel Fitzwilliam's behest."

Charlotte shuddered.

"I will tell you, Eliza, it was unbearable! I was on the verge of marching down myself and making them give the laudanum to the poor man. Hearing Mr. Darcy cry out like that..."

She shuddered again.

Intense shame swept through Elizabeth. *She had slept through all that?!* She reached for her own teacup and warmed her fingers against the warm porcelain.

"Mr. Darcy called out your name a few times, if you must know," Charlotte added, piercing her with a knowing look.

It only made Elizabeth feel worse.

She sipped the tea to ease the queasiness in her stomach.

"Is Mr. Darcy sleeping now?" she asked.

Charlotte nodded.

It did not make her feel any better.

It was much later in the afternoon when Colonel Fitzwilliam came to find her.

Elizabeth was in the small garden outside the cottage, sitting on a bench and trying (and failing) to read a book she had found inside the house.

"Miss Bennet."

She looked up.

"Darcy is awake now."

They stared at each other for a moment. The Colonel appeared flustered and a tad embarrassed. She was still exhausted.

"Charlotte told me."

"I meant the laudanum has started to wear off," Colonel Fitzwilliam said. "If you wish to say something to Darcy, now would be a good time."

Elizabeth frowned as she stood up. Something about his words bothered her. "What are you saying?"

Colonel Fitzwilliam sighed and rubbed a palm over his face.

"The physician—Dr. Goodman—is not certain if Darcy is out of the woods. If he will…"

Elizabeth's eyes widened. "You mean…"

Colonel Fitzwilliam nodded.

Tears pricked Elizabeth's eyes so hard, the throb spread all over her nose and face. She turned away at once, blinking furiously to compose herself.

"Miss Bennet?"

"Just… give me a moment, sir."

When she knew she had mastered herself, she turned back.

"I am ready now."

Chapter 31:

STRANGERS

It was different when Elizabeth walked into Mr. Darcy's room the second time.

For one, the physician and his valet were both present.

For another, his eyes found hers as soon as she walked in.

...only to flicker uncertainly to Colonel Fitzwilliam's who was right behind her.

"Dr. Goodman, Clarence," Colonel Fitzwilliam said to the other two men. "If you could give us a few moments?"

Once it was just her and the Colonel in the room with Mr. Darcy, Elizabeth approached his bedside. Apprehension thrummed through her. Her heart hammered in her chest.

"Fitzwilliam?" Mr. Darcy rasped. He was partly groggy, but still aware.

He was still looking uncertainly at her.

"It is alright, Darce. Rest easy," the Colonel said, settling into the chair vacated by Dr. Goodman. "Miss Bennet has come to see you."

Mr. Darcy continued to stare at Elizabeth. And then quickly looked away. She wondered if he was embarrassed, though it was hard to tell with all the bruising on his face.

"Hello, Mr. Darcy," she said, searching his face. "I hope you are feeling better."

"Like death warmed over," Colonel Fitzwilliam quipped from his post.

Mr. Darcy glared at his cousin. And then he looked at her again. This time she knew he was blushing underneath it all.

"Hello, Miss Bennet..." he rasped with difficulty. Then he tried to clear his throat and winced. "Thank you for your... kind wishes."

They stared at each other.

Elizabeth could feel warmth spreading across her face. But she tried to stay calm on the outside.

"Did you... just arrive?" Mr. Darcy asked.

Elizabeth frowned.

She glanced at Colonel Fitzwilliam. He was watching the two of them like a hawk, but said nothing.

"Yes," she said. An odd sensation was beginning to sprout within her.

Something was not right.

"Earlier... in the morning," she added.

Mr. Darcy tried to nod, and then winced again, closing his eyes for a moment in exhaustion. "Thank you... for visiting..." It appeared he had fallen asleep.

Elizabeth could feel the familiar prickle behind her eyes and nose.

...but this time, it came at the heels of an awful knowing in her gut. A disconcerting, gathering despair.

Did he not remember?

Surely that could not be true?

"I shall leave you to rest..." Elizabeth whispered, allowing herself one last look of Mr. Darcy's familiar face.

She steeled herself.

Then she dipped a quick curtsey for the Colonel, before quitting the room.

Chapter 32:

ENDINGS?

"Are you well, Eliza?"

The cart bumped and swayed along the road. They were making their way back to Hunsford.

"Yes," Elizabeth said, giving Charlotte a half smile.

It was the middle of the day with bright sunshine around them and the chirping of cicadas in the grassy knolls. They were traveling much faster than before. Elizabeth fixed her gaze outside the window. There was not a single cloud in the sky.

...by early evening, they reached the parsonage.

That was when her tribulations truly began.

First, it was Mr. Collins.

He was so incensed about what Charlotte had done that he forgot himself for a while and berated his wife in front of everyone, including the cart driver. And then he berated Elizabeth. *She* must have been the bad influence on his biddable wife!

Then, Mr. Collins dragged them both to Rosings, presenting them to Lady Catherine as if offering up lambs for a sacrifice.

The lady—not being one to throw away any opportunity to terrorize and dominate—did what she did best: attempt to subdue such ungentlewomanly behavior.

She was especially displeased with Elizabeth. *For, who was she—a wholly unrelated person to her family's great stature—to meet Darcy before her own daughter could?*

Of course, Colonel Fitzwilliam was not spared in her rebukes. But since the man had not chosen to return with them to Hunsford, he, at least, was spared the incessant thumping of Lady Catherine's staff on the floor and the barrage of her vitriol.

They were questioned quite thoroughly after that.

Where was Mr. Darcy? What was his condition? What happened after he woke up? How much laudanum was he being given? Dr. Goodman could not possibly be a good physician if he had chosen to give Darcy that little laudanum! Mr. Hanson—Miss de Bourgh's personal physician—would have never allowed such an oversight!

How could they have traveled all that way without enquiring the name of the village!?!

Elizabeth bore it all in silence and terse replies.

She did not care what Lady Catherine—or Mr. Collins for that matter—thought of her. She knew they were ridiculous. But she feared that life would become difficult for Charlotte once she left for Longbourn.

...because that was what was decided in the end.

That she was to go.

After all, Lady Catherine, in her superior wisdom, knew it was best if Miss Elizabeth Bennet went home straightaway. *All the better to keep such unrelated persons out of matters wholly unconnected to them!*

But, of course, Elizabeth was not to go straightaway.

There were letters that needed to be sent.

First, to her Uncle Gardiner in London—to send a carriage to convey her to the Gardiners' home in Gracechurch Street. It was always the plan, and Mr. Collins did not see why *he* needed to spend money on hiring a post to rid himself of *such an incriminating presence in his house!*

The other letter was addressed to her father at Longbourn, complete with Mr. Collins' blistering recommendations on how to take one's daughter in hand.

After all, if Mr. Bennet had done so from the start, Miss Elizabeth Bennet would not have turned *him* down in marriage—how preposterous!—and would have had the benefit of Lady Catherine and his guidance to prevent *such undutiful and scandalous undertakings!*

Mr. Collins ensured Elizabeth—and everyone else—knew the exact contents of his letters by reading them aloud during breakfast the very next day. He wished them to know that he had burned the midnight oil to accomplish said task. All because he believed it was his duty to Lady Catherine *and the reputation of his household!*

He also wished them to know that he would not stand for his dear, innocent Charlotte being spirited away into the night. *Never again!*

And so it was only natural that two days hence, Elizabeth found herself once more alone with Charlotte with a big pot of tea between them.

Her plot to escape her friend's scrutiny had failed.

"Eliza, something is troubling you," Charlotte said, sitting down on the long settee beside her. "Will you not tell me?"

Elizabeth stared at Charlotte for a moment.

Thoughts flew through her head.

And then...

—all of a sudden—

...the dam she had built inside to hold back all the distress of the last few days finally burst.

She turned away instantly as a rush of tears began to fall down her eyes.

"Oh dear!"

Charlotte tried to draw her into a hug but Elizabeth resisted... before she allowed herself to be wrapped in a tight embrace. She tucked her face over Charlotte's shoulder.

"Oh, Charlotte... I do not know..." Elizabeth said, through her tears. "I think... Mr. Darcy does not... he does not remember anything!"

Charlotte rubbed her back softly. "My dear girl."

Elizabeth felt as if her heart would split in two. She hugged Charlotte tighter.

"I do not know why I care so much. If I even should," she said in a rush. "What a wretched thing this is! I wish I had never met him!"

"Shh... shh... all will be well." Charlotte stroked the back of her head.

"You will not believe this, Charlotte..." she said after a bit, her voice suddenly stronger. "But, for all that effort to write Miss Darcy's letter, I left it behind in Mrs. Ronald's cottage." Bitterness flooded her mouth. "I forgot all about it!"

"Shh... shh..."

"All I could think of was how Mr. Darcy looked at me," Elizabeth said. "As if I were some lukewarm acquaintance come to extend unwanted wishes. Some great interloper..."

"My dear, shh... that cannot be true. Only Lady Catherine would say such a thing," Charlotte said. She patted Elizabeth's back. "I am certain Mr. Darcy was pleased to see y ou."

"Oh, Charlotte, you do not know..." Elizabeth squeezed her eyes shut as more tears streaked down her face. "You should have seen how Colonel Fitzwilliam was watching me. As if all his suspicions had been confirmed. Oh..."

The two friends sat in that manner for the longest time.

But once Elizabeth's tears dried, Charlotte promptly handed her a cup of sweet tea. It had lost most of its warmth though. "I shall have Janet bring us a fresh pot."

Elizabeth simply drank down the entire cup in one breath. She was parched.

"Here, have some more," Charlotte said, filling the cup again and adding another generous helping of sugar to it.

Elizabeth winced. "Charlotte–"

"Just drink it, Eliza. You will see."

It was awful. Too sweet. Too cold. But Elizabeth did feel better afterwards. Enough that when Charlotte returned to her seat after instructing Janet, she said what was truly weighing on her heart.

"Could you write to Colonel Fitzwilliam about the pages I left behind?" Elizabeth asked. "I do not think he will bother with anything I send. And Mr. Darcy's physician... Dr. Goodman said that he may not live..." She twisted her fingers into fists. "I do not want... all that effort to be for nothing."

Charlotte looked at her kindly.

"I will do it."

Elizabeth nodded and fixed her gaze on her hands as they rested over her knees. Her eyes were prickling again.

"Then... I believe all shall be well."

A Year Later...

Chapter 33:

OAKHAM MOUNT

E lizabeth was darning some clothes for Longbourn's tenants in the east parlour when Mrs. Bennet burst in through the door. She was overwrought with excitement.

"Mr. Bingley is returning to Netherfield!" Mrs. Bennet cried. "Mr. Bingley is returning!"

Stunned silence greeted her for a moment.

Then, Kitty and Lydia shrieked.

Excited words flew through the air, even as Elizabeth and Jane sat frozen. Both for different reasons.

"Jane! Jane! Is that not wonderful news?" Mrs. Bennet asked, plopping herself on the chair next to the eldest of her five daughters. "I always knew Mr. Bingley would return. You could not have been so beautiful for nothing!"

Jane blushed. "Yes, mama."

"Oh! I never doubted him," Mrs. Bennet continued, contradicting every behavior and word of the last many months. "And now Mrs. Dudley tells me that they have reopened the house. He shall be here any day now! Oh, what good times we shall have!"

Mrs. Bennet fanned herself with her handkerchief.

"I shall remind him that he owes us a dinner at Longbourn. Oh yes, I shall." She fanned herself faster.

"There will be three full courses—and better than any he might have anywhere in the King's lands! Oh, what a marvellous day it is! Kitty!" She screeched. "Open the windows! It is awfully warm in here! And bring Mr. Bennet from the book room. We have much to discuss..."

Elizabeth stifled the sharp pain in her heart as Mrs. Bennet's effusions continued.

She closed herself off to the almost-festive atmosphere in the parlour. After all, it was not as if Mr. Bingley's friend would be with the Netherfield party this time. *That* would be too farfetched to expect!

Eight months had gone by since news reached her that Mr. Darcy was well and truly out of the clutches of death.

...a full year since what had happened in Rosings.

Yet she had not heard a word from him.

Not a line to acknowledge the strange experience they had shared.

Not even a wish to maintain a connection—of any kind—with her or her family.

Elizabeth discreetly slipped out of the parlour so as not to draw her mother's attention. She did not wish to partake in the foolish celebrations.

She could not bear it.

The next day, Elizabeth left early for her morning walk and decided to climb to the top of Oakham Mount.

She was struggling to stifle the feelings that the news yesterday had brought out of her. She wished to stuff them back in her heart and lock them tight.

...perhaps the perspective from the top of the hill would help her regain her equanimity.

And so, there she was.

At the top of Oakham Mount.

Minding her own business. Gazing at the cotton clouds drifting over the pasture lands. Wondering when spring would finally breeze into Hertfordshire...

...when she heard the distinct sound of boots climbing up the inclination somewhere behind her.

Elizabeth turned.

And froze.

"Miss Bennet?"

It was Mr. Darcy.

He raised his top hat in a smart bow. A greeting. There was a small smile on his lips. Partly hesitant. Partly warm.

Elizabeth turned away instantly and squeezed her eyes shut. Her heart pounded.

"This cannot be real..." she whispered to herself, trying hard to compose herself.

"Miss Bennet?"

But there was that sound again!

Him calling her name. And it was closer.

Sudden fury scorched through Elizabeth's veins. She turned around to find Mr. Darcy standing only a few feet away from her.

"Why am I seeing you?" she asked sharply.

Her heart twisted in her chest as she searched his face. He paled.

"I... had hoped..."

"No, stop this!"

Elizabeth turned away once more and fixed her gaze on the distant church steeple and the herd of sheep grazing on a field. "I cannot bear it..." The little white dots shifted and moved over the green.

"If I have done something wrong..."

She whirled around again. "The only thing you have done, Mr. Darcy, is utterly ruin my sanity!"

Then she strode straight at him, glaring her displeasure and...

...collided with a hard body!

Elizabeth screamed even as Mr. Darcy's arms came around her, and her own hands latched onto his shoulders to stop herself from falling.

"Miss Bennet!" he said in shock.

Their eyes locked. She stared at him, frozen dumb. Still very much in his embrace. Neither looked away.

"You are not an apparition...?" she asked softly. Emotions flared inside her, alongside intense disbelief.

Mr. Darcy searched her eyes. His dark gaze spoke volumes, touched as they were with sorrow and something else. Something familiar.

"No."

Instant mortification raced through Elizabeth. *Like fire!* She pushed away from him at once, looking everywhere but at him.

"I apologize, Mr. Darcy, for my lack of decorum. I–"

She glanced at him and looked at the ground again, blushing furiously. "I... shall go now."

Elizabeth walked around him and strode away, wishing the ground would open up and swallow her whole. *Of all things that might have happened!*

"Wait, Miss Bennet!"

She did not stop.

Heaven's above!

The burn of mortification was almost overwhelming.

"Please, Miss Bennet, wait!"

She heard, rather than saw, Mr. Darcy run after her. But her feet would not let her stop.

"Please... Elizabeth."

She gasped when Mr. Darcy's warm hand caught hers. She came to an abrupt halt. He did not let go.

Instead, he tightened his hold around her fingers.

"Will you not look at me?" he asked.

Too close.

Elizabeth stared at the tree tops and blinked her eyes furiously as they prickled with unshed tears. The memories rushed back.

The cherry trees. The copse. The letters. The awful cups of sweet tea. Standing across from each other in the quiet silence of her room. The feel of his hand in hers...

...just like right then.

"Thank you for keeping me company when I..." Mr. Darcy's voice became strained. "When I was in between life and death."

Elizabeth whirled around and stared at him.

"You remember?"

Mr. Darcy did not look away from her, even as their fingers interlaced.

"Yes."

Elizabeth did not know what else to do than continue to stare at him and feel the tears roll down her face.

"I thought I would..." Her voice broke. She looked at the ground between them. At the dirt, gravel, and scattering of grass. Somehow their joined hands entwined even more. She tried to speak past the lump in her throat.

"I thought... I would be the only one to remember," she said. "That I would be the only one... burdened with it until the end."

More tears flowed down her cheeks. Elizabeth squeezed her eyes shut.

"No, never," Mr. Darcy said, drawing her closer. She could feel his fingers brushing away her tears. Holding her face.

...that was when Elizabeth realized just how lonely she had felt all those months.

To carry the strangeness and unbelievable reality of what they had experienced, all alone. She leaned into his hand, raising her own to press it to her cheek.

"Elizabeth..." Mr. Darcy whispered.

She opened her eyes.

Their gazes locked.

...and then Mr. Darcy pulled her into his embrace and kissed her.

Chapter 34:

True Love's Kiss

Their lips moved softly against each other's at first.

Brushing. Tasting. A reverence.

Elizabeth could feel a warmth growing within her heart. Expanding like the sun.

"I love you," Mr. Darcy whispered against her lips.

They kissed again.

It was as if they wished to recover the lost time. Unable to let go. An ever increasing intensity.

Everything their hearts wished to say was parsed through their lips and embrace. Everything unspoken.

When they finally pulled apart, they gazed into each other's eyes. Elizabeth smiled. Radiance was spreading through her being.

Then she gave him a mock stern look.

"Well, Mr. Darcy, I hope you intend to marry me after taking such liberties with my person."

He blushed, but did not release her from the circle of his arms.

"Madam, if there ever was any doubt about that, let me rectify it right away. There is no one else I would like to spend the rest of my life with than you."

Elizabeth felt her cheeks heat.

Like the warmth of a fireplace against the cold.

"I would like that," she said softly.

She leaned forward and touched her lips to his once more.

Epilogue

It was only once they were walking back from Oakham Mount, hand in hand, that Elizabeth asked what was burning in her mind.

"How did you remember?"

Mr. Darcy's hand tightened around hers immediately.

"I thought I had dreamt it all."

"Oh."

He squeezed her hand again. "Once I found the letter to my sister, I realized it may not have been a dream."

Elizabeth looked to the ground as they walked. Emotions churned within her.

"I left those in the cottage and did not remember until I was halfway back to Hunsford. I am sorry."

She remembered how she had cried until Charlotte had assured her that she would write to Colonel Fitzwilliam. Mr. Darcy entwined their fingers until she looked up.

"Richard found them and kept them safe."

She nodded.

Charlotte had told her as much in a letter after she had returned to Longbourn.

"...but he did not return them to me until last week."

Elizabeth stopped walking.

It was as if someone had dropped a boulder on her heart. The ache she had carried in her chest for months returned. And grew.

Agitation thrummed through her.

"Why?"

She hated how strangled her voice sounded.

What if the Colonel had never returned the pages to Mr. Darcy?

They faced each other. He did not let go of her hand.

"He did not think it was necessary."

There was pain flashing in Mr. Darcy's eyes. Elizabeth stared at their joined hands. Her eyes prickled as he raised their entwined hands and held it against his heart. She could feel the thuds within his chest.

"I could not stop thinking about you," Mr. Darcy said. "The memories... what I thought were dreams, kept coming back to me."

He held their joined hands more firmly against his heart.

"When I walked under the cherry trees at Pemberley, or sat on a garden bench at a friend's estate, or watched two women drinking tea... I could only think of you. It was incessant."

His heart was beating faster.

Elizabeth looked up. Raw anguish was on his face.

"Almost everything reminded me of you. I could not write a letter without the oddest feeling that something was left unfinished."

There was a sheen in his eyes.

"Richard caught on eventually and confessed to me about you, and what he called your peculiar claims. That was when it dawned on me."

Mr. Darcy reached out and cupped her cheek, his thumb brushing a line of fire along her skin. Elizabeth sucked in a breath. Neither looked away from the other.

"I remembered our last conversation in Mrs. Ronald's cottage," he said. The sheen in his eyes were tears now. "The feel of your hand in mine..."

The gravity between them had grown excruciating.

The distance, unbearable.

They leaned into the other, and kissed again.

Elizabeth closed her eyes as more tears rolled down her face, a deep thrill shivering up her spine. Her arms wound over his shoulders and into his hair. His top hat fell to the ground.

Mr. Darcy wrapped his arms around her waist, drawing her even closer.

The kiss deepened, until they were left gasping. Breathless.

"My dearest Elizabeth."

Fin

About the Author

Author Austen Commission by Tara Hatton

Morgan Blake writes Austenesque variations of Pride & Prejudice
that are sometimes steamy, sometimes not. Satire is the name of

the game and happy ever afters the goal! Morgan is a cat friend, perennial night owl, and tropical girl who prefers winter clothes.

I hope you enjoyed reading The Cherry Trees of Rosings. If you did, please consider leaving a review.

If you'd like to gift a copy, this book is available to purchase in paperback.

Coming Soon: Next

A Pride & Prejudice Variation

Can a bad first impression give way to love?

A Spirited Kiss

by Morgan Blake

Releasing in 2026

When Fitzwilliam Darcy of Pemberley—he of ten thousand pounds a year, and subject of instant speculation at the Meryton assembly—casually declares (in the earshot of the lady in question) that she is "not handsome enough to tempt him", he probably did not expect said lady to march right up to him and tell him in the face to "rest assured" she *was not* interested in him either.

Thus, ensues a battle of wills of cutting remarks and frosty greetings. One stretching weeks and weeks, right in the middle-of-nowhere Hertfordshire.

For, if there is one thing Elizabeth Bennet of Longbourn hates more than the constant banshee-wheeling of her marriage-minded mother, it is a man who believes himself superiority itself. *Probably someone who could not be bothered with politeness if his life depended on it!*

But are Darcy and Elizabeth truly what they seemed to each other at first? Or, is it just a case of bad first impressions and fine English stubbornness?

Let there be drama! Let there be intrigue!
And let there be—*for certain!*—a fiery romance with heated debates, buried family history, unreliable relatives, and surprising kisses of the earth-shattering variety.

Tread carefully, dear readers. This *Pride & Prejudice variation* will leave you fanning yourself with hectic abandon and reaching for a tall glass of water. Happy ever after, guaranteed.

Coming Soon in 2026

Visit www.morganblakeauthor.com
and sign up for Morgan Mail (newsletter)
All subscribers receive a free Lizzy x Darcy novelette
(to enjoy with your next cup of tea.)

SIGN UP TO RECEIVE
<u>AUTHOR MORGAN BLAKE'S NEWSLETTER</u>
BE THE FIRST IN THE KNOW
ABOUT BOOK RELEASES,
GIVEAWAY BOXES & MORE.

ALSO AVAILABLE:
(SUBSCRIBER EXCLUSIVE DOWNLOAD)
LIZZY X DARCY
NOVELETTE

WWW.MORGANBLAKEAUTHOR.COM

Printed in Dunstable, United Kingdom